CALL IN THE DOGS

THE GREEN COUNTRY SERIES #2

CHARLIE AMOS

This is a work of fiction. Names, places, characters and incidents are either the product of the author's imagination or are used fictitiously, and any resemblance to any actual persons, living or dead, businesses, organizations, events or locales is entirely coincidental.

Publishing Coordinator – Sharon Kizziah-Holmes
Cover Design – Jaycee DeLorenzo

WRITE THE WEST PRESS
an imprint of Paperback Press, LLC
Springfield, Missouri

ISBN -13: 978-1-970560-15-2 (Paperback)
ISBN -13: 978-1-970560-16-9 (Hardback)
ISBN -13: 978-1-970560-17-6 (eBook)

Dedication

For River, now we are even.

Acknowledgments

I would like to thank everyone who purchased my first book. Your feedback and support encouraged me to write this second book for you. Thank you for forgiving my amateur mistakes in book one and taking this journey with me. I will forever strive to deliver you a better story than the one before.

I want to thank the Western Writers of America and its members. They keep the American West alive through song, literature, and historical accounts. As well as the ragtag group that meet in Eureka Springs, Arkansas every October for the Ozark Creative Writing Conference. Those two groups carry the torch first lit by early man who stood up and captivated those gathered around firelight.

Finally, I would like to acknowledge the Divine providence that placed me here at this time. Who provided the path that I chose giving me the experiences needed to give you this story.

Chapter 1

"Soil yourself. I don't care," the marshal grumbled, adjusting himself on a sack of mail.

Bill Kirby's eyes narrowed. The leg irons and handcuffs clanked as he tried to make himself comfortable on the rail car floor.

"Now, because the train is full, I allowed you to ride in here. But I can't have him making a mess," The mail-car clerk protested.

"Get a pullman porter to clean it up. Besides, he's just moaning, trying to get out of those chains."

"Perhaps. There is a pan in the corner for such bowel relief."

"How about it, Kirby? You need to go?" The marshal leaned forward, his arms on his knees.

"Unchain my hands so I can do my business." Kirby raised his arms, tugging the chain tight between his wrists.

"No, you'll have to make do." The marshal pointed toward the pan in the corner.

Kirby slowly rose, using the wall as support. The rail car rocked and bumped. Standing on sore stiff legs, he lost balance. Stumbling forward, he caught himself against a large wooden crate.

"I can barely walk with these chains, let alone relieve myself," Kirby grumbled.

"Something you should have considered before getting yourself caught." The marshal leaned back on his pile of mailbags.

Kirby backed into the corner, and the chains clanged against the pan as he loosened his trousers.

"Oh, dear God," the mail clerk murmured.

Gases escaped confinement and filled the mail car with a noxious odor.

"Crack the door," demanded the marshal.

"It is against regulations. The chain of custody must be preserved, and cargo secure." The mail clerk spoke through a handkerchief held to his face.

"Regulations, hell, I'm a federal officer. I'll open it myself." Tossing his coat aside, the marshal stood up. With his back to Kirby, he opened the door. Cool, fresh air rushed in, and so did the noise from the train rolling along the tracks.

"What have you been eating?" the marshal shouted.

With one hand holding his trousers, Kirby ran at the marshal's back. Nearly tripping he allowed his momentum to knock the marshal off balance and giving him a shove. Scrambling to grasp the doorframe, the marshal hit the rocky slope and rolled down toward the brush along the track.

"Lie down and shut up, or I'll toss you outside." Kirby closed the door.

Complying, the clerk fell to the floor.

Kirby searched the marshal's coat and found a push key and soon had the chains off him. He bound the mail clerk's hands and looped leg chain through a handle of a large crate.

"Where we at?" Kirby demanded.

"Seligman, Missouri maybe," the mail clerk said nervously.

"Where's the next stop?"

"Cassville."

"Take on any letters or put any off there?"

"No. Not until Sedalia," the clerk said in a half cry.

"Good."

Kirby searched the car. The marshal's coat would fit him. Rummaging through the clerk's carpetbag, he found a tin container. From it, he pulled bread and quickly ate it along with a chunk of cured ham.

"Got any weapons?" Kirby spoke with a mouth full of food.

"No. No, sir."

"Not even a knife?" Kirby nudged his ribs with a boot.

"Yes. A pocketknife."

"Just lie there. Don't move." Kirby pulled it from the man's pocket along with a watch and thirty dollars then shoved everything into the pocket of the coat he wore.

Finding a crock on the counter, he used the dipper and drank. Water droplets fell about the motionless clerk, running into his ear. Returning the dipper to the crock, Kirby let out a belch.

Canvas bags with seals and reinforced leather bottoms sat in a row on a shelf above the counter serving as the clerk's desk.

"What's in those bags?" Again, Kirby nudged the clerk with a toe of his boot.

"Mail."

"Why are they all on the shelf and not over there?" Kirby pointed to the sacks the marshal had been lounging on.

"It's mail. Certified mail." The clerk struggled speaking.

"What's them seals mean?"

"Means it is certified."

"Stop being so mealymouthed." Kirby grabbed one

of the bags and dropped it on the counter.

"It's only certified records. Receipts from ledgers."

"Let's have a look." Kirby cut open the canvas. Money, more than he ever seen before, spilled out.

Seven more bags sat on the shelf, and he quickly opened them all.

"Are you going to kill me?" the clerk asked in an uneven voice.

"Not if I can help it. Just know, I will slit your throat if you try anything."

The clerk wasn't likely to try anything chained to a wooden crate.

Kirby picked up the carpetbag, discarded clothes too small for him, and shoved the money into it.

"You say Cassville is the next stop?"

"Yes. Yes, sir."

"Here's the deal. I'm getting off the train in Cassville whether I kill you or not."

"Please don't kill me." The clerk closed his eyes.

"You're doing good, kid. All you have to do is stay quiet. Now I'm going to stretch you out some so you won't thump around and make noise." Kirby squatted and tousled the clerk's hair as if he were a child. He took the man's spare shirt and tied his already-chained hands above his head to an iron ring in the wall. As an afterthought, he grabbed a mailbag and stepped back to the stretched-out little man.

"Ow." The clerk winced.

"About as comfortable as I can make you." Kirby lifted his head by his hair and shoved a sack of mail under it like a pillow.

Kirby continued to rummage through the car for anything useful. If his luck held, he figured he had several hours until the train reached Sedalia and authorities would be notified.

His clothes were ragged, but the marshal's coat fit

well enough. He snatched the clerk's hat off a peg and tried it on. Too small. He tossed it aside. The marshal's hat had gone with its owner.

"What time does the train get to Cassville?" Kirby asked as he opened his new watch.

"One."

"Speak up, kid. Can't hear you over this racket."

"One," the clerk shouted.

"Almost one now. Stay quiet until Sedalia, kid. All I ask of you." Kirby snapped the watch closed.

"Yes. Yes, sir."

"Best not take a chance." Kirby stuffed a handkerchief into the clerk's mouth and tied a second one around his head to hold the first in place.

Picking up the carpetbag, he went to the front door of the car. Sliding the lock open, he stepped onto the running board and waited as the train slowed. He now had his freedom with more money than most people made in a decade or a lifetime. The law would search for him, but they had hunted him before.

"Spring Creek. The little foreigner was traveling to Spring Creek in the Cherokee Nation. Little Kansas they called him."

Kirby would have been well out of the country, if not for the little foreigner. He had stopped at a camp last September in hopes of getting a fresh horse. He knew the U.S. marshal was following him. He didn't know how close, though. While trying to take a roan mare from a little foreign man, he was delayed when the man put up a fight. Before he could teach the man a lesson, the US marshal got the drop on him. He spent all winter waiting in the Fort Smith federal jail for court and his transfer to federal prison. He had decided he could wait a decade to kill the little man with the roan mare. Now, he wouldn't have to wait that long.

The train slowed as the running board he stood on

came even with the platform. He hopped off and made a few quick strides. Just another traveler in a hurry clutching a bag. He blended in with the people at the depot. Soon, he was down the street.

Chapter 2

"Queenie is out in front," Turon Turtle said, reaching over to put a stick on the fire.

"Stump is close behind," Ounce Pathkiller grunted.

The men spoke in hushed tones as the hounds tracked the fox. The two Cherokee had been speaking mostly in English for the benefit of the third man, Levi, known to most in the area as Little Kansas. A nickname he picked up while cowboying out West where he had met the Cherokee Turon Turtle.

Born and raised in a poor family in Poland, fox hunting was foreign to Levi Kuratowski. Only the rich had hounds. Here he sat with two Cherokee, a hemisphere away from home.

"How can you tell which dog is in the lead?" Levi asked while staring at the night sky.

"Each dog sounds different. Has its own voice, as people do," Ounce replied.

"Yeah, Queenie has a sharp tone. She's the boss. Now, Ounce's dog Stump has a deeper bark, as if he's in a well. Also, he sounds as though he's way behind Queenie," Turon added while grinning and giving Ounce a sidelong glance.

Ounce spoke in Cherokee too quick for Levi to

understand the words, but he understood the gesture.

"Stump will catch that old fox, you'll see," Ounce added.

"Better be an old fox if Stump is going to catch it." Turon pulled a tobacco pouch from a coat pocket and unrolled a small paper between his fingers.

Ounce once again grunted.

"I heard you priced Stump to Ned Foreman for fifty dollars," Turon said, carefully dumping tobacco on the paper then rolling a cigarette.

"Yeah," Ounce said while accepting the tobacco pouch and papers from Turon.

Reaching for a burning stick to light his cigarette, Turon asked, "What makes him worth fifty dollars?"

"I traded two twenty-five-dollar fighting roosters for him." Ounce built his own cigarette.

The smiling Turon reignited his stick and leaned over to offer Ounce a light. "Why don't you breed Queenie to Stump? Get some pups," Levi asked.

"I would rather she got snake bit," Turon said, tossing the stick into the fire.

An owl let out his night call not far away. Levi thought nothing of the bird. The two Cherokee went quiet. Owls were harbingers of death, giving warnings for the Cherokee. Minutes passed before anyone spoke.

"I should probably get back to the wagon and store," Levi said.

Since coming to the Cherokee Nation, the quiet Jewish immigrant Levi had become a small-time celebrity. A celebrity brought on by Turon's exaggerated stories about their trip from Texas driving Turon's Hereford bull home. A brief misunderstanding between Levi and four Cheyenne over the ownership of the bull turned into a full-out battle. A haphazard capture of an outlaw who tried stealing Levi's horse on the Cimarron River became a quick-draw gunfight.

After their employer Mr. Hatcher decided to sell his holdings in the Cherokee Outlet and move back to Texas, the cowboys found themselves unemployed. Turon decided to buy a bull and build a cattle herd. Levi, who dreamed of owning a store in Kansas City, settled on building a mercantile business near the crossroads of two well-traveled trails on the banks of Spring Creek in the Cherokee Nation.

Levi felt he owed Turon and his family a great debt. They had helped him obtain a trading license in the Cherokee Nation. Despite Turon starting a new life with his wife Lorelei, they pooled their money to buy two wagonloads of goods. These Levi sold under a brush arbor and lived out of his wagon. Taking his meals occasionally with Turon's family who owned a farm down the creek, Levi had grown close to them. Turon's sister Ruth had taken interest in the venture as well. Turon had joked that he wasn't sure if Ruth's interest was in selling store goods or Levi himself.

"I was told to bring you home." Turon too stood.

"You were?"

"Ma is worried you are working too hard and missing too many meals. Ruth seems concerned about you too."

"Toe and Lee may need help," Levi replied.

"Them Hogshooter boys won't miss you for a few hours."

The pitch of the dogs changed. Queenie bayed, followed by Stump.

"The fox has gone to ground," Turon said. "Put out the fire. Let's call in the dogs. It's time to head to the house anyway."

Turon walked over to his horse and retrieved a large cow horn hanging on his saddle. He walked a dozen steps toward the hounds. Lifting the horn to his lips, he took a deep breath. A blast from the horn started low, increasing ever louder until the sound broke in a crack. Two more times he did this, reminding Levi of the shofar, also known as the horn of Abraham.

Daylight was threatening the night sky as Turon and Levi rode west with Queenie trotting alongside. Ounce and the dog Stump had left them earlier to return home near Clouds Creek. Riding into Turon's home place, lantern light shone through the windows. The farm was bathed in twilight and they could make out the buildings.

"That's Tall's wagon out front." Turon motioned with his chin.

"He must be back from Tahlequah." Levi squinted to see the wagon.

Tall Maul was a white man who had years before married a Cherokee woman. Height gave him his first name. His real name and place of origin was unknown. The Cherokee who had come to know and trust him never asked.

Turon unsaddled his horse and turned him into a cedar-pole pen with the other horses and mules the Turtle family owned. Levi loosened the cinch but left his roan mare saddled.

A deep voice greeted Turon and Levi as they approached the front porch of the log house.

"You boys look like you've laid out all night with the dry stock." Tall Maul stood with hands resting in the rafters of the porch.

Turon was tall for a Cherokee, just over six foot. Tall had half a foot over Turon and towered over the five-foot-two Levi.

"Been running some hounds with Ounce over by Flint," Turon said, shaking hands with the big man.

"Your father said you were running dogs. Yesterday evening, I was worn out and decided to stop here for the night, or I would have ridden out and joined you."

"How did you make out in Tahlequah?" Levi shook hands with the man towering over him.

"Not as good as I have in the past. Furs were down. Barrel staves did okay." Tall reached out and thumped Levi on the chest with the back of his hand. "Little Kansas, I've got just what you need."

Levi and Turon followed Tall to his wagon. Sitting in the bed was an ornate cast-iron stove and a dozen feet of stove pipe.

"Made by the Charter Oak Stove Company. I figure you will need one in the store." Tall leaned an arm on the edge of the wagon bed.

"How did you come by it?" Levi asked.

"Miller and Sons lost their trading license with the Nation. The sons struck out for the boomer settlements last spring, and the old man left to join them. He had his whole shop loaded in wagons except this stove. Anyway, he was cursing because his help quit him. He hollered at me as I was passing by on the wagon. Ordered me to get some help and load his stove. I told him if he wanted it just to pick it up. He said any man who could lift it into a wagon by himself was welcome to it. Well, this interested folk within earshot. Soon bets were placed on whether or not a man could lift it." Tall reached a hand to the stove and rocked it. The wagon wood and springs creaked under its weight.

"I'm surprised the Miller's lasted in business this long. The old man was never very friendly," Turon commented.

"He got even more unfriendly. A pretty good-sized crowd had gathered around by then. Including the boys who had just quit the old man. I just walked over to where they had left the stove. Squatted down and got ahold of it. Stood up, walked about ten feet, and set it on the back of my wagon. The crowd cheered, and the old man yelled in protest. The crowd reminded him of the deal he made, and he left yelling insults to the entire Cherokee Nation."

"It must weigh a quarter ton. You don't need it?" Levi asked.

"We have a good stove. I was thinking you might need it. You can pay me, or we can trade for credit at the store. Say, fifty dollars?"

Levi reached out and shook Tall's hand. "I'll take it."

Lorelei stepped outside and called for breakfast. The men walked to the house. Tall entered first followed by Levi.

Turon's sister Ruth locked eyes with Levi and offered him a cup of coffee, she smiled. He took it and looked away.

Turon's father John sat at the table and motioned for Tall and Levi to have a seat. Turon and Lorelei entered the room, and Turon joined the other men at the table.

Tall ate with an appetite equal to his height. Near the end of the meal, after he had cleaned his plate of gravy and leavings, he reached for a jar. He drizzled sorghum on his plate, mixing it with butter, then sopped it up with one of Lorelei's biscuits.

"I almost forgot. You might find the front page interesting." Tall pulled a copy of a Tahlequah newspaper out of his coat pocket and slapped the paper onto the table by Levi.

"Escaped." Levi read the headline and paused before continuing. "Wild Bill Kirby who was recently sentenced to ten years at the federal penitentiary in Detroit, Michigan emancipated bondage Tuesday last. The audacious escape was achieved when Kirby overpowered Federal Marshal Powell Stuart and threw him out of the SLSF mail car near Seligman, Missouri. Stuart was later found alive with several broken bones and a severe head injury. Kirby not only managed to escape but did so with an estimated twelve thousand dollars in payroll and secure funds from the mail car. Kirby's arrest in September by Deputy Marshal Bass Reeves was aided by Levi Kuratowski, better known as Little Kansas, who subdued the outlaw after an attempted horse theft. Little Kansas, who is new to the territory, operates a trading post on upper Spring Creek. Kirby remains at large, and his whereabouts unknown." Levi set the paper down after reading it aloud.

"Those funds weren't so secure." Tall motioned with a coffee cup toward the paper.

"By gum," Turon's father said, after letting out a low whistle.

"Couldn't ask for better luck." Turon reached for the paper and scanned the headlines.

"Luck?" Levi asked.

"This is free advertising. Now, even more people will know about the store."

"Won't Kirby know where to find Levi now?" Ruth asked with concern.

"Eh, I doubt the man can read," Turon said. He will be too busy with his newfound wealth." He turned the paper over.

"I remember Kirby. The jagged scar across his jaw and the way he glared at me from the prison wagon the last time we seen him in Tulsey Town."

Tall's face fell in disappointment as Lorelei picked up the platter of remaining biscuits.

"Better save some to take Toe and Lee. They might appreciate them," Lorelei said while setting the platter on the kitchen counter.

As she placed them in an old flour sack along with some cured ham, Tall's expression brightened.

"I'll be more than happy to drop the biscuits off to

them." Tall stood finishing his coffee. "I have to deliver Little Kansas his stove."

"Very kind of you, Mister Maul." Lorelei added extra biscuits to the sack.

"What about Bill Kirby?" Ruth sounded irritated.

"Stick to your knitting, girl," Ruth's mother told her.

Frustrated, Ruth did not say another word. She helped clean up. Her twelve-year-old brother, Choogie, followed the men out onto the porch. He squatted against the wall, watching the men.

"Do you think Kirby will come here searching?" Levi asked no particular person.

"He would be a fool if he did." Tall was the first to speak.

Turon's father spoke in Cherokee, and Turon answered in kind. Tall spoke in Cherokee briefly.

"Little Kansas, you do not need to worry. Kirby is known in these parts. We will spread the word, and folks will be on the lookout for him. Any sightings of him, and people will come and let us know." Tall spoke in a reassuring voice.

"Keep the shotgun at hand. Also, you should carry your Navy Colt when you travel." Turon stood cross-armed, watching out from the house across the farmstead.

Levi scanned the ridge across the creek.

Lorelei came out onto the porch, carrying the sack of food.

"I better take those boys their biscuits. You can ride with me, Little Kansas, and we can decide where you want your stove."

"Sure, Tall. Let's go." Levi nodded.

"Lorelei" Tall bent over, making a long sweeping gesture with hat in hand. "As always it was a pleasure, and thank you for the breakfast and hospitality of the Turtle family."

Chapter 3

The sound of hammers echoed as Tall and Levi approached the store site. Bare rafters exposed to the sky were slowly resembling a roof as Toe and Lee hammered the nails home, securing the decking.

"You will be ready for shingles soon enough," Tall remarked.

"I've more cedar to split. Should have enough shingles by tomorrow."

As he said it, Levi thought he should have been sleeping instead of staying up all night listening to the hounds.

The building was simple. Twenty-four feet wide and forty long. A false front faced the south with a porch ten feet deep and the width of the building. Levi had argued against the false front and the large windows in the front of the store. Turon insisted they needed the light from the windows, and the false front would give it a sense of prosperity.

Under a large oak tree halfway between the store building and the creek, two ancient Cherokee men sat watching the progress and commenting to each other in hushed tones. Neither spoke English and, although Levi always greeted them, his growing Cherokee vocabulary was not enough to engage in conversation. The two old men would nod and occasionally smile.

Tall hailed the old men, and they spoke and nodded. It amazed Levi, the ease with which he spoke Cherokee. Although his towering height could be intimidating, his easy manner disarmed people, and they would soon open into conversation.

"How long did it take you to learn Cherokee?" Levi asked when they reined up in front of the store.

"Well, I got hungry. Hunger is a good incentive to learn a language."

"I understand. Much like I learned to speak American." Levi nodded, thinking about how he had to learn English when he came to the United States.

"Of course, the Turtles are feeding you too well for you to ever learn fluent Cherokee. I myself didn't get fluent until I married a Cherokee girl." Tall eyed Levi. "How big are your living quarters in the back of the store?"

"Ten by twenty-four feet," Levi said.

"Plenty of room for a bachelor. Might get small with a wife and family," Tall remarked.

"I am a bachelor."

"For now. You don't have a girl back across the water?" Tall asked.

"No. I barely owned my clothes when I left Poland. No girl would have shown interest."

"Ruth, she seemed concerned about your safety this morning. I bet she could teach you some Cherokee."

"She has been teaching me a little," Levi admitted then started to blush when he caught Tall's meaning.

Toe climbed down a ladder from the roof. The athletic Lee eased down a rafter, dangled a moment, and landed softly on the floor of the store.

Tall removed two biscuits for himself and handed the sack to Toe who nodded approvingly. Toe apologized to Lee there wasn't enough for him. Lee furrowed his brow, mumbling. Toe laughed then handed the sack to his brother to share what was plenty.

The Hogshooter brothers had used Levi's cook fire spot and pot to make a pot of coffee. Levi retrieved it and some cups.

"We should have enough one-by-six boards to finish decking the roof today," Toe spoke with a mouthful of food.

In broken Cherokee, Levi said he would split more shingles.

The twin brothers laughed, and Toe made a comment in Cherokee directed at Tall.

"He said they were good on split squirrels, but what they needed were more cedar shingles." Tall grinned.

"Shingles, split shingles." Levi repeated in Cherokee.

Tall spoke in Cherokee at length as Toe and Lee laughed.

"What are you saying?" Levi asked.

"Just commenting on how well your Cherokee is coming. Toe thinks Ruth could teach you some more." Tall sipped the coffee.

"I better get to it." Levi stood up and finished his cup.

Beside the store building, a pile of cedar logs had been de-limbed and cut in eighteen-inch lengths. Levi picked up a froe and tested the edge. He placed a chunk of wood on a cross section of log. Taking the froe, he sat it on top of the wood edge down. With a mallet in one hand, he hammered the froe, driving it down. He continued hammering down making precision slices through the cedar. The dark heart of the center would last years if properly fitted on the store's roof.

Levi stopped briefly to wave goodbye to Tall as he drove his wagon to his place on Saline Creek in Bull

Hollow. Levi remembered the stove and felt guilty he did not help unload it. However, he soon fell into a rhythm. He trimmed, split, and stacked shingles. Once, a man stopped him to buy a few items from under the brush arbor. The rider didn't stay long, and Levi went back to the shingles. Trim, split, stack, and repeat. The hammering stopped, but Levi continued. Lost in his own world of thought.

"Shouldn't you be carrying a gun?"

Levi turned to see Ruth sitting on a black-and-white pinto; her expression was stern and two sacks hung from the saddle.

"Hello, Ruth. What brings you out?"

"Ma sent some lunch over. Shouldn't you be carrying a gun? I could have been the outlaw Kirby." Ruth repeated her question with a raised eyebrow.

"You are prettier than he is." Levi was surprised at his own words. "Toe or Lee would have yelled had he rode in."

"Come eat." She climbed off the pinto and carried the food over to the porch.

He led the pinto near where his own roan was staked out and tied him to a low limb of a post-oak tree. Ruth had a shotgun hanging from the saddle. He took it and carried it over to the store. "You came armed." He leaned the gun against the wall.

"Someone needs be ready." Ruth arranged food items on the porch.

"I can't work with a pistol on me." Levi eyed the food.

"You can't work if you are dead." Ruth picked up two fried pies and walked to the giant oak the two older Cherokee sat under.

She joked with the old men. In just a few minutes, they talked more to her than they had to him in two weeks. She left the men laughing and came back to the store building. Levi returned his attention to the food.

Toe and Lee sat with their backs to the wall. The two like mirror images of each other. Ruth questioned them in Cherokee, and they answered in serious tones. Levi gathered enough of the conversation to understand Tall had told them to watch out for strangers and Kirby.

"You shouldn't worry about him. Before he was captured, he wanted out of the country. He will go out West now."

"You don't know that."

Ruth's gaze penetrated his very soul.

"I'll keep a gun handy." Levi said, hoping the subject would change.

Trace chains rattling caught Levi's attention. A Cherokee man drove a mix-matched team of mules. A woman in her twenties sat beside him, and four children rode in the wagon bed.

Ruth greeted the family in Cherokee as they pulled up beside the brush arbor. Levi went over to help them with their purchases, although Ruth did much of the talking. She knew the family, but Ruth was kind and generous to most people. She laughed and made others laugh, reserving her sternness and judgment for Levi.

Two more families stopped by, as well as a few lone riders. Men inspected the building and women visited with Ruth who handled the transactions. She had been helping Levi enough with the Cherokee customers, she was better at selling goods than he was. He soon went back to splitting cedar shingles.

Late in the afternoon, the Hogshooters' hammers stopped, leaving a fully decked roof. Once they installed the shingles, he would have a functional building. It still needed windows and a door. In a few days, he could pick them up at the depot in Siloam Springs, Arkansas some fifteen miles to the east.

"We are going home for the day," Toe said while

putting on his coat.

"You did a good deal of work." Levi sat the froe and mallet down on the piece of crosscut log.

"You did too. May be enough." Toe gestured to the stack of shingles.

"Might." Levi nodded, a little surprised at how much he did.

"We will be back tomorrow." Toe waved and jumped behind Lee who was riding a plow horse barebacked.

Levi was watching the brothers ride off to the north when Ruth came up close beside him. "Are you finished?

"O kurwa." Startled Levi jumped a bit.

"What, that Cherokee?" Ruth smiled.

"Nothing."

"What does it mean?"

"Well. It means... It means to be surprised," Levi finally said.

"I could have been a bad outlaw."

"Maybe you could, but you haven't turned to a life of crime yet."

"You need to pay better attention to your surroundings," Ruth scolded.

"Why should I? You are doing a decent job of playing lookout."

"Are you finished?" she repeated.

"With the shingles? I am. It's still early. Could be someone will come by the store."

"I'll wait. You may need help with a customer."

Levi followed her up the steps into the store.

"It really seems like a store now." She glanced up into the rafters where the decking blocked out the sky.

"Need to build some shelves, and a counter will go here." Levi waved a hand.

"The living quarters are too small. You will need more room," she said, going to the back of the store to the narrow room.

"It's big enough." Levi was defensive at the comment.

"What about your wife and family?"

"What wife and family? I'm a bachelor," Levi said.

He never saw it coming. Ruth's right fist caught him. A stabbing pain shot through his arm, and it went numb.

"Ow, what are you doing?" Levi rubbed his arm.

She embraced and kissed him.

His first reaction was to pull away, but he soon abandoned the notion. No longer feeling pain in his arm, he held her close.

She pulled away slowly after a few moments, smiling. "You're going to need to add on to the living quarters."

"I am?" Levi slowly regained composure.

"After we get married, I'm not going to live in a storeroom forever. I want a house."

"M-marry me?"

"Why, yes. Of course I will," Ruth said.

"No, no it wasn't a proposal. Marry me, but why?

"Do you not think I'm pretty?" Ruth frowned, but the corners of her mouth trembled threatening a smile.

"You are beautiful. I just haven't thought about marriage," he said defensively.

"You never will. It is why I must decide for us. You might be good at building and running a store, cowboying, and catching outlaws, but you need help when it comes to asking a girl to marry you." Ruth stood with her hands on her hips.

"Are all Cherokee this quick to marry or just your family?" Levi crossed his arms.

"We just know what we want when we see it."

"Do I have a choice in the matter?"

"You can always run away. Try your luck somewhere

else."

Before Levi could respond, his roan mare nickered and he heard a rider approaching. They went to the front of the store.

"It's nearly finished." Turon reined up in front of the store, a Henry rifle resting across his saddle.

"Getting there. We can start putting shingles on tomorrow," Levi said, noticing the two older Cherokee had disappeared from under the oak tree.

"Little sister, Momma wants you back to the house." Turon motioned with his chin to Ruth.

"Sure, Turon." Ruth side-eyed Levi as she walked by him to get the pinto.

"Might as well close shop and ride in with us, Little Kansas. Supper will be ready after a while." Turon adjusted himself in the saddle.

"I appreciate it. I've got a few things I could do here." Levi's eyes never left Ruth as he watched her climb onto the pinto.

"It can wait. I've been to visit Ounce. He's going to come over in the morning. Between all of us, we can put the shingles up and maybe get some shelves built. Choogie can fetch material." Turon glanced at the pile of shingles.

"Sounds like you just want to keep an eye on me," Levi said.

"Truth is, we all have grown attached to you. Also, wouldn't be a bad idea to get this building finished. Redbuds and plum bushes will bud soon. Rains will come after."

"Let me cover the tables and put some stuff away." Levi walked to the tables and secured the store goods the best he could.

Ruth rode the pinto close to the porch and lifted the shotgun up from where Levi stood it against a porch post.

Levi climbed into the wagon bed where his belongings were neatly arranged. He pulled a canvas sack from under a blanket. From it, he took out an old Navy Colt revolver. He checked the cylinders and shoved it into his right boot.

“Good. You should carry it more,” Ruth said.

“I can’t hit anything with it, but I thought it might make you shut up.” Levi mounted the roan mare.

Turon grinned and nudged his bay toward home. Levi followed with Ruth riding beside him. Her laughing eyes irritated Levi a bit, but he soon forgot her mocking glance. She sat straight in the saddle, her body in rhythm with the pinto as she moved him into a trot.

Chapter 4

Levi stopped splitting shingles long enough to watch the two old Cherokee take their seats under the oak tree. He sat another piece of cedar on the cross section of log. Toe and Lee's hammer strikes echoed in the mid-morning air. Ounce carried shingles to Tall. Tall had parked his wagon close to use as a scaffolding where he handed shingles to Turon who in turn handed them to Toe and Lee. The boy Choogie looked for fallen nails and found every excuse to climb the roof.

"You'll fall and break your neck if you ain't careful," Tall warned the boy.

Levi did not mind doing the groundwork and avoided heights. He split more shingles in case they ran out. He could always sell what he did not use in the store. Turon had told him they needed to build a horse and mule barn anyway. It too would need shingles.

Tall's wife visited with Turon's mother as they helped Ruth and Lorelei prepare a noon meal near the brush arbor and wagon. An occasional rider or wagon came by, and Ruth would manage the sales. Hammer strikes echoed mixed with the swings of Levi's mallet sinking the froe into the cedar wood.

Finally, no more cedar chunks lay about. Only

shingles. At a tug on his sleeve, he turned to see the two old Cherokee men standing close. The one who tugged on Levi's shirt spoke softly in Cherokee.

"He says you need a well," Ruth said.

"A well? There is a creek down there."

The old man talked for several minutes. He motioned to the other Cherokee who held a fresh-cut persimmon branch trimmed into a large Y shape.

"He is going to dowse a well."

"He's going to what?"

"They have been here for sixty years and say you can't depend on the creek."

"How does this dowsing work?" Levi set the froe on the cross section of the log.

Ruth talked to them. The one with the persimmon branch held it with his palms up the fork balanced by fingertips. The main branch stuck out in front of him. He walked around in front of the store, and the stick occasionally tipped down and back up. He made several slow circles, always coming back to one spot. The last pass, he came toward the tree a few steps. Halfway between it and the store front, he stopped. The tip of the persimmon switch tipped down and shook a little.

He spoke in Cherokee to Ruth. She nodded and turned to Levi who had watched the exhibition.

"He says you should dig here. Twenty-four feet down, you will find all the water you will ever need."

"He guarantees water?" Levi asked.

"You can bank on it, Little Kansas." Tall came over to the group.

"Does it get that dry here? The water seems so good."

"It can." Tall pointed a finger at the oak. "Makes sense the tree got as big as it has if a spring is down there."

The old man stuck the forked stick into the soil

marking the spot. He smiled and pointed at it then spoke in Cherokee.

Tall laughed.

"What did he say?" Levi asked.

"He asked if you are willing to bet your strawberry roan mare on whether the water is down there." Tall grinned.

"Don't take the bet, Little Kansas." Turon walked up and looked down at the stick.

Turon's mother called out for the noon meal. Tall, who had just been standing beside him, was first in line where the women set the food out.

"Would you say grace, Tall?" Turon's mother handed him a plate.

He bowed his head. It was a short prayer, and he repeated it in Cherokee.

By the middle of the afternoon, the roof had been shingled. Ounce and Levi had built shelves for the inside, and Ruth and Lorelei moved items from the brush arbor and wagon into the new store.

"You can make improvements as you go." Turon flicked a splinter out of his thumb with a knife. "For now, you've got a store, Little Kansas."

"We have a store. I couldn't have done it without you." Levi inhaled the smell of the lumber.

"You can be the one who runs it. I've got cattle to tend."

Turon walked outside and Levi stood envisioning what he had left to do. He still needed the windows and a proper door. A ceiling required installing as well as interior walls. For now, he had a store.

"What are you thinking about?" Ruth came into the store.

"All I have to do." Levi turned to face her.

"All *we* have to do," she corrected him.

"We?" he asked.

"You are slow to learn Cherokee. I expect it will take me years to teach you. Once we are married, we will have more time."

Levi shook his head.

"I think June will be good for a wedding. Just before the Green Corn Ceremony." She arranged some fabric on a counter.

"What makes you so sure I'm the one you should marry?"

He still had a tough time deciding whether she was serious or teasing him.

"Before Turon left to work out West, he promised me he would return one day and bring me a present. He brought me you."

Ruth moved closer to him.

"I thought he gave you that Osage pinto?" Levi's heart pounded in his ears and his knees trembled.

"You. You are who I choose." Ruth jabbed Levi with a finger, bringing a stab of pain to his chest.

Before he could protest, she wrapped her arms around him and kissed him, causing their teeth to knock together. As quickly as she had embraced him, she let go, turning abruptly. Her ponytail swung with force equal to her affections, slapping him across the face. Ruth went out to join the rest of the building crew who were eating fried pies and drinking coffee under the brush arbor.

"I thought I better grab one for you before Tall ate them all." A floorboard creaking near the door announced Lorelei's arrival. She set a cup of coffee on the counter and handed a pie to Levi.

"Thank you." Levi took a bite.

"We have come a long way since you and Turon came into our camp in the canyon." Lorelei commented.

"Yes, we have."

"I don't have to say this. We are family. I know not by blood, but you are like a brother to me." Lorelei causally crossed her arms.

"I feel the same way."

She moved close and lightly hugged him around the shoulders then took his head in her hands. Tilting it down slightly, she kissed his forehead.

"I am happy for you. I know you will do well here." She released him and moved to the door.

Turon met his wife at the door, and the two exchanged a glance before he came inside, making the same floorboard creak.

"You didn't come in here to hug me too, did you?" Levi took another bite of the fried pie.

"I hadn't planned on it." Turon eased himself onto the counter, swung his legs off the side, then continued. "I was in a store in Orchard City once. They had a cracker barrel. We need to get one."

"What did they cost?"

"I just remember they were tasty and salty. Made me thirsty. I figure we can keep a barrel out. Loafers will eat them, and you can sell cups of coffee once they are thirsty."

"Sell perked coffee? I can see selling beans, even grinding them." Levi blew steam from his mug. "Selling cups of coffee will never work. People won't stand for it."

"You're the store clerk. I'm just a cowboy." Turon shrugged.

"Cowboy and part store owner."

"I may sell my part to Ruth. She has interest in the store, seems to like clerking, or at least the clerk."

"She is good with customers."

"You're not Cherokee, but I think of you as much of a brother as Choogie. I speak for Ma and Pa and all of us. Should you decide Ruth suitable to be a wife, then we would not object."

Levi stared at the floor.

"If you decide not to marry Ruth? Well, it has been nice knowing you." Turon hopped off the counter.

"Would you run me off?"

"Hell, no, Little Kansas. Just said you were like a brother. Now, Ruth doesn't feel the same way. If you turn her down, she may kill you. I would miss you but, in time, I would get over it."

"Marry Ruth or be killed are my only options?" Levi lifted the coffee cup to take a drink, but it was empty.

"You can run, go to sea. Maybe give Australia a go."

"I made one voyage across an ocean." Levi shook his head. " I will not make another."

"We can bury you on the little rise to the northwest where you can look down on the store you built." Turon grinned.

"You and your sister must be working on this together. Does me being a Jew bother anyone?"

"I've got a cousin in Tahlequah who married a man from Missouri. We don't hold it against him. You will be fine," Turon continued. "Just keep in mind—the family is agreeable to the arrangement, should it happen."

Levi stood, not saying a word.

"Want some more coffee?" Turon reached for the empty cup.

"Yeah," Levi managed to say.

"Two pennies." Turon laid his hand out, palm up.

What?" Levi came out of his trance.

"Two cents should be about right for a cup of coffee."

"Makes as much sense as anything else in this place."

Chapter 5

If the residents of Nebo, Arkansas noticed the man in the dark suit, they didn't show it. He rode down the street on a sorrel mare leading a black mule laden with the gear of a man outfitted to sleep outdoors. Also tied to the pack was a carpetbag.

Bill Kirby did not stop to visit anyone in the little village. He would have avoided Nebo altogether, but he'd feared riding around it would draw suspicion. He had done his best to change his appearance. The recent capital allowed him finer clothes. The scar on his jawline was common among men who labored outdoors.

He touched the brim of his hat as a lady's glance met his. West of town, he passed plowed fields lying like patchwork with hay meadows and fruit orchards. Ahead was Beaty Creek and the last known whereabouts of his old friend. Kirby did not trust many. He was not sure he trusted Blue Tate.

"Excuse me, can you tell me where the Tate farm is located?" Kirby asked a young man in overalls who was driving a Jersey bull down the road toward Nebo.

"You mean Molly O'Brien's place," the farmer said after a careful study of Kirby.

"Maybe. Seems like he married a widow with a name similar."

"Well, not sure they stood in front of a preacher. Can't say they ever found a body to match her departed husband. But that's where you will find Blue, saw-milling with Molly."

"Where's the O'Brien place?" Kirby tried not to let his impatience show.

"Keep riding until you reach the creek. Downstream to the place on the left. A run-down look to it."

"Much appreciated." Kirby urged the horse and mule west, leaving the man with his bull.

As the farmer described, the place Kirby rode into had a run-down appearance. Trash and debris lay about the yard in front of the house. A wagon sitting on wood blocks needed a new wheel, the hub assembly in pieces. Chickens pecked and scratched throughout the junk and trampled grass.

"Are you collecting taxes?" A sharp voice came from the open door. "I already paid up."

A crimson-haired woman emerged from the little shotgun house. She was shorter than most, with a broad face burned by the sun, she wore ill-fitting clothes, and her ample proportions caused strain on the fabric and thread.

"Is Blue Tate here?" Kirby reined up at the edge of the yard.

"Are you the law? He was acquitted on those charges. Cost me two bred sows. You have no hold on him now." She ran a hand through coarse, unkept hair.

"It's all right, Molly." A blue-eyed man came around the corner of the house.

"Hello, Blue."

"Bill." Blue nodded.

"Bill? Bill who?" Molly asked.

"Bill Hawkins, ma'am." Kirby removed his hat and

set up his alias.

"I never heard you mention a Bill Hawkins, Blue," she said sternly.

"It's all right, Molly. Bill, let's turn your horse and mule into the barn lot. Molly, how about you fix something to eat for our guest."

"If you want something to eat, fix it yourself. I ain't running no boardinghouse." Molly went back inside.

"I thought you would have lit out to the territories by now, Bill," Blue said once they were away from the house.

"It's what I aim to do. I have unfinished business over in the Nations to take care of first."

"I see."

"I need to borrow your eyes." Kirby dismounted.

"My eyes?"

"There's a little foreigner over in the nations running with some Cherokee. I think one of them has a farm on Spring Creek or in the area."

"There's thirty miles of drainage from the prairie to where Spring Creek dumps into the Neosho. What have my eyes got to do with it?" Blue opened a gate to a corral.

"The foreigner and them Cherokees are close with the marshals. They know me there. If I go in there searching, they are liable to find me before I can find them." Kirby loosened the cinch on his saddle.

"I don't know. Molly expects me to start plowing soon. Should have already started."

"I need a week out of you, maybe five days. How does one hundred dollars sound?" Kirby stared at Blue, seeking a reaction.

"One hundred dollars? Where did you get that kind of money?"

"Never mind how I got it."

"This foreigner? He owes you something?"

“You could say he does. Less you know, the better.” He thought about it and added, “The less Molly knows, the better.”

“She is sharp. Hard to trick.” Blue looked over his shoulder to the house.

“Fine woman you have there.”

Kirby did not really think so, but he was trying to placate Blue.

“She bristles up some, but rub her behind the neck just right and she calms down easy like.” Blue turned back to Kirby.

“I also need a place to lie low. Not here. I wouldn’t want any neighbors to see me.” Kirby scanned the area.

“I know a place. There’s a cabin near where Coon Creek hits the Spavinaw. The family left for Texas last fall. No one has taken it over yet. I use it some when I need to get away from Molly. She has her moments.”

“Tell her I’m hiring you to show me around the country for a week or so. Say I’m buying cattle.” Kirby lowered his voice.

“Could work,” Blue said.

“You can tell her later the hundred dollars was your commission.” Kirby awaited Blue’s response.

“Let me get my hat and a blanket. Gather a few things.” Blue trotted to the house.

A few minutes passed, and Kirby was lounging on a feed sack in the barn. Rats had torn a hole in the corner of the sack. Oats spilled onto the floor. Kirby was thinking of the futility of rodent control when he heard a shout from the house.

“You’re a lazy worthless leech.” Molly was three steps behind Blue. “What in the hell do you know about buying cattle?”

“All I need to know is who has the cattle. Bill is the one doing the buying.”

“We have fields needing plowed! Harnesses need

mending!" She caught up to him. "And you want to gallivant around the Nations with a bunch of blanket asses."

Blue saddled his horse as Molly continued to berate him. Kirby tightened his cinch and mounted, grabbing the mule's lead rope. Both the horse and mule lunged away from the redheaded woman screaming a profanity-laced tirade against him. Kirby, struggling to keep his seat in the saddle and a hand on the mule's lead rope, rode out of the pen and turned west.

Blue caught up even with him a few minutes later. His hat pulled down low and his head set forward, he never looked back as if to do so would turn him into a pillar of salt.

"She can get excited sometimes," he finally said, still looking forward.

Kirby had no response. He had little experience with a full-time woman. What could be so appealing it would make a man tolerate such behavior?

Spavinaw Creek started near Nebo spread into a broad valley where it crossed into the Cherokee Nation. Coon Creek came from the south and where the two streams met a ridge formed between them. On a bluff, a single-room cabin stood. The door had the letters G T T carved into it.

"Gone to Texas." Blue swung down from the saddle.

"Why'd they leave?" Kirby surveyed the small well-built cabin and nearby pole corral.

"The Cummins never made a crop. They always had money, though. Both the Benton County sheriff and the Indian police got to noticing the number of missing horses matched the sets of horse tracks coming up this ridge." Blue loosened the cinch on his saddle. "They got greedy. They also got word they weren't long for the country. The Anti Horse Theft Association has really gotten a toehold hereabouts."

Kirby nodded. The AHTA were a membership group of vigilantes. They filled the gaps in the loopholes laws and courts seem to have occasionally. Some of the members were not much better than the people they chased.

"Harder and harder for folks to make a living these days." Kirby walked over to the edge of the bluff to view Spavinaw Creek and the valley below.

"What can you tell me about this foreigner?" Blue asked.

"His name is Levi or Lemuel or something similar. They call him Little Kansas. He's a small man. Kid really."

"What exactly do you want me to do if I find him?"

"Just find him. Let me know where I can find the little bastard." Kirby began unsaddling the sorrel.

Blue moved over to the mule and began to unload his burden.

"I'll take care of the pack. He's a biter." Kirby quickly took the carpetbag from the mule.

"All right." Blue eyed the mule who stood with his head down as calm as could be.

Kirby carried the carpetbag and a bedroll into the cabin. Blue went to a stack of firewood and moved some sticks. From a void, he pulled a crock jug. Kirby heard the pulling of a cork.

"Molly can't have any, or she gets careless. If I want a drink, I got to sneak off." Blue offered Kirby the jug as he stepped out of the cabin.

"You got any more of this stashed around?" Kirby wiped a droplet from his chin and sucked a finger.

"Ample supply, for emergencies and such. I'm partnered on a still." Blue took the jug and sat on the porch.

"Good business?" Kirby eased down on the porch and leaned against the cabin wall within arm's reach of

Blue.

"At times, revenuers keep the pressure on. The trade is steady. Worth the risk I suppose." Blue handed the jug to Kirby.

"What does Molly think about it?" Kirby took another sip and set the jug down between them.

"She isn't exactly a temperance member. She likes the money. You appear to be living well, Bill. Fine clothes and all."

"I had some luck. I've only one small task to take care of, and I'm quitting the country." Kirby removed his hat and ran his fingers over his scalp, scratching the back of his head.

"The foreigner?"

"Just can't let it go." Kirby reached for the jug. "I want to see him hurt."

"It's a lot of country to cover. Be hard to find one man, foreigner or not." Blue pulled a plug of tobacco from a coat pocket, along with a knife.

"The Cherokee he was running with had one of those red-and-white face bulls. Herefords they are called. High-bred son of a bitch."

"There aren't many of those in this country. Find the bull and you will find him." Blue tucked a slice of tobacco in one side of his mouth. "Acting as a cow buyer might be as good of cover as any."

"When you find him, just let me know."

"Can you spare some expenses? I can pick up a few supplies in Cherokee City in the morning. Figure I can ride over to Salina and down the Neosho then back up Spring Creek." Blue spat a brown stream of tobacco juice landing just off the porch.

"This should get you by." Kirby separated five dollars from a coat pocket and handed it to Blue.

Blue stuffed the money in a pocket and took another drink.

Chapter 6

"Selling coffee by the cup?" Tall asked as he set a heavy crate in the wagon.

"He said the crackers will make people want to drink, and we charge by the cup." Levi dragged the crate to the front of the wagon bed.

"Turon is part horse trader." Tall set another crate at the wagon's tailgate.

A depot agent approached. "Mr. Kuratowski, they are unloading the rest of your order now. Will you be able to move it today?"

"We have a second wagon over there. Should all fit." Levi motioned to his wagon with the mix-matched team he borrowed from Turon.

"Very good, I'll have the boys place it on the south end of the platform." The depot agent returned to his duties.

"I appreciate you helping me get all this in one trip, Tall." Levi stacked a crate in the front of the wagon box.

"It's a pleasure. The ice cream alone is worth the trip." Tall placed a barrel on the wagon's tailgate for Levi to pack away.

They soon had both wagons loaded. Tall's Percheron team tugged the trace chains evenly as they left the depot. Levi's older and smaller wagon followed.

Siloam Springs, Arkansas sat a few miles from the border of the Cherokee Nation. Its depot was the nearest place Levi could receive his store goods. Downtown had the area's premier and only ice cream parlor.

Finding a spot along Sager Creek, they halted their teams and set the brakes. The two men walked toward the Crown Hotel. A few townspeople eyed them. Tall's towering height, beard, homespun clothes, and worn beaver hat contrasted Levi's five foot and two inches still wearing the clothes of his prairie cowboying days.

"The circus in town?" a passerby said in a low voice to another townsperson.

"Just wind, Little Kansas. Never mind them."

Tall stepped onto the boardwalk below Shelby's Ice Cream Parlor.

A bell at the top of the door rang as they entered. Men and women wore tailored and store-bought clothing. Everyone stopped and stared at the David and Goliath duo.

"Right here is a table." Tall removed his hat and motioned at a little table for two at a window facing Mount Olive Street.

"Hello, welcome to Shelby's." A young lady in a starched blue dress and white apron approached.

"Good day, ma'am. How are you on this fine day?" Tall smiled at the girl.

"I am blessed. Would you two care to hear our special?"

"By all means." Tall adjusted his chair, and his knees bumped the table.

"We currently have peach ice cream. The peaches from Orchard City, last year's preserves."

"Sounds good to me," Tall said. "Two scoops for myself."

"And you, sir?" The girl turned to Levi.

"One scoop, please."

"Certainly." The girl stepped to the counter and returned with two glasses and a pitcher of water.

Tall sat with his hands folded, making the already-small table appear smaller. Table conversations had returned to the other patrons. Lace curtains hung in the windows. A glass display held cakes and cookies. Levi caught movement and a boy approached the table. Dressed in short pants and socks up to his knees. His coat buttoned up to the top.

"My mother says you are a giant." The boy stared directly at Tall.

"Your mother is right, boy," Tall's deep voice rumbled. "Fee-fi-fo-fum, I smell the blood of a mother's son."

The boy's eyes widened.

"Richard!" a woman's voice snapped.

"Apologies, gentlemen. He knows better." The mother gathered her son, scolding him for leaving his seat.

"Perfectly fine, ma'am. He's no bother." Tall smiled at the boy.

People nearby chuckled.

"I suppose you do look like a giant compared to me." Levi took a sip of cool water.

"Takes all kinds to run the world. We all got our place."

"Here you go, gentlemen. Is there anything else I can bring you?" The girl placed glass dishes of peach ice cream on the table.

"No, ma'am. That will do." Tall rubbed his hands together.

Levi savored the ice cream. It was a luxury he would have normally avoided but having use of Tall's wagon and team plus Tall, he considered it a needed expense.

"You got to ease through it, or you will get a headache." Tall held the spoon like a surgeon and methodically ate the frozen dessert.

"We should build an icehouse next. Save ice during the colder months and store it." Levi scraped the side of the dish with his spoon.

"We could. Bull Hollow is deep. Not much sun. We could dig into a north facing slope and rock it." Tall carefully maneuvered his spoon over his beard and under his mustache. Ice cream clung to the tips of his mustache despite his efforts.

"Something to consider."

"This stuff always makes me thirsty." Tall drank the glass of water in one gulp.

The trip to Siloam Springs and back took most of the day. Tall and Levi had left before daylight. It was evening when the two wagons pulled up to the store. Ruth walked out on to the porch when the wagons approached.

In front of the store where the persimmon branch had been stuck into the ground, Toe Hogshooter appeared like a groundhog, followed by Lee.

"Almost took you two for critters."

Grinning, the two climbed out of the hole and started helping unload the wagons.

"There is stew on the stove once you are finished," Ruth announced.

Soon they had the two wagons unloaded. The crates would need unpacking, and items sorted, but Levi could do it later. They each held a bowl of stew. Levi blew steam from a spoonful and walked to the well the twins had started digging that day. Tall followed, ignoring the temperature, and spooned it into his mouth.

"You boys did a fair amount of work." Tall peered into the hole.

"Looks big around," Levi commented.

"Has to be. The floor and sides will need rocked. Keep it from caving in." Tall shoveled a spoonful of stew into his mouth.

"Do you think the old man is right? Water will be twenty-four feet down."

"I wouldn't doubt him. If he says the water is there, it's there."

"More stew?" Ruth called from the porch.

"Yes, ma'am." Tall moved quick and held his bowl out for her to ladle more into his bowl.

"Hello at the store!" A big voice boomed out of nowhere.

A Cherokee riding a bay plow horse hollered as he kicked the big horse into a jarring short lope toward the storefront.

"It's one of them Foreman boys from down on the river," Tall said between spoonfuls.

"Ned Foreman," Ruth clarified.

"My woman done had a big bull baby, boy I tell you." The beaming Ned jumped from the horse onto the porch.

"Congratulations. Want a bowl of stew?" Ruth offered.

Ned shook his head and turned to Levi. "Little Kansas, need some tobacco, and a big jar of them peaches."

"Sure, Ned." Levi stepped onto the porch and into the store.

"Big bull baby, that long." Ned held his hands apart like he was describing a fish to Tall and the Hogshooter brothers.

"How's Maggie?" Ruth asked.

"She's doing fine, done up and about," Ned walked into the store.

"Need a little flour, Little Kansas." Ned pulled a flour

sack from his waistband and Ned shook coins loose. They landed on the wood plank.

Levi slid the proper amount toward himself and the remaining back toward Ned. Then he placed a jar of peaches and the tobacco on the counter. He took the empty sack and filled it with flour from a barrel. Twice, he weighed it. The second time, the needle wavered and settled a hair over five pounds. “Is there anything else I can do for you?”

“Come see my new bull baby.” Ned shoved the tobacco into a coat pocket and slapped him on a shoulder. “He going to be a big boy.”

With a running leap, he landed on the back of the plow horse with the flour and peaches under an arm.

“Got to get home. Come see us.” Ned drummed his bare heels into the sides of the plow horse.

“I better make tracks too; you boys want a ride?” Tall asked Toe and Lee.

As Tall and the Hogshooter brothers left for home, Ruth stood on the porch and Levi began to move a crate inside the store.

“Do you ever rest?”

“I do, some.” Levi stopped.

“It’s late, I should go home soon.” She gathered the stew bowls and carried them to a nearby tub of water.

“I will saddle your horse and my mare. I need to take your father’s team back to him anyhow.” Levi checked the horizon and fading light.

On his way to saddle the horses, he reached below the wagon seat and pulled his revolver from a sack. Checking the cylinders, he then stuck it into his high-top boot.

“Glad you are taking Kirby serious,” Ruth said with some satisfaction.

“He’s halfway to Mexico by now. This is for panthers or wild Indians.”

"Sure. Still stew left if you are hungry later or in the morning." Ruth went to the pinto.

"Thank you. You didn't have to go to the trouble."

"No trouble, I thought it best. Toe and Lee had worked hard. You and Tall had a big day. Couldn't expect you to cook for them." She stuck two fingers behind the cinch, testing to see if it was tight before stepping into the saddle.

"I can cook." Levi was defensive.

"No doubt you could survive. Good luck getting Tall or the Hogshooter brothers to help you though." She toed a stirrup and with grace, climbed on the pinto.

Mumbling, Levi climbed onto the roan mare.

"Let's get you home before your mother starts to worry," Levi finally said and turned his horse toward the Turtle farm with a smiling Ruth riding beside him.

"I smell smoke." Levi turned in the saddle.

"Pa and Turon are helping some of the neighbors burn. Pa said the wind is right." Ruth motioned with her chin toward the west.

In the fading twilight, they rode up a rise and could see the fire line on the horizon to the west. The fire burned slow since the wind had laid with the approaching darkness. They held their horses and watched the flames creep eastward.

"It must be a mile wide." Levi adjusted himself in the saddle and made a sweeping glance to the west.

"Probably at least a mile."

"Why do they set the prairie on fire?" Levi studied the horizon.

"They set the woods on fire too. It kills the little brush and sprouts. Makes the grass and berries grow," Ruth explained.

"Does it ever get out of control and away?"

"Only if we don't burn. Burning keeps the grass tender. Good for cows, deer, and turkeys. If we didn't burn it, the brush would take over and crowd out the grass. Competing against the brush for sunlight, the blackberries, huckleberries, and strawberries wouldn't grow."

"Well, we need the berries and grass."

Two riders approached.

"*Siyo*, Little Kansas, Sister." Turon rode in, closely followed by Choogie on a mule.

"*Siyo*, Choogie, are you keeping an eye on your big brother? He will do to watch, you know," Levi greeted the smiling boy.

"Choogie, why don't you take the team home and Ruth too."

"I want to set the fire," Choogie challenged.

"If Ma doesn't need you, hurry back and you can still help." Turon said with a hint of authority. "Best get Ruth and them horses home."

"Come on, Choogie, I'll help you with the horses."

"Choogie, if you don't get back tonight, come to the store tomorrow. I got some hard candy in today." Levi handed him the lead lines for the team.

Slumping in the saddle, Choogie took the horses and followed his sister into the pending darkness toward home.

"What do you have in mind, Turon?"

"Light a backfire from the creek back around the store. Take these and soak them in the creek." Turon handed him two gunny sacks.

"Soak?" Levi took the sacks.

"Get them good and wet. I'll start a fire. We will let it burn a strip then come in behind it and put it out. Make a fire break so when that gets here, it will stop." Turon pointed to the approaching fire line.

Turon gathered a handful of dried grass into a torch. Striking a match on his pants, he lit the grass. As it burned, he walked and dropped the torch to the ground igniting the dormant vegetation. Once the handful had burned down, he would drop it and gather another handful. Lighting the bundle on the expanding flames, he repeated the process.

Levi soon had two dripping-wet gunny sacks and was at Turon's side.

"Here, take a sack and smother the flames on this side. Like this." Turon smothered the fire with the wet sack and, in places where the grass was short, he simply stomped it out.

"All right." Levi nodded.

"I'll keep setting fire back north, circling in behind the store. Then down to the creek on the far side."

The slow fire spread out from where Turon set the burns. Levi followed, stomping and smothering it out. Once Turon had set his semicircle of flames, he joined Levi in creating an arch of burned ground protecting the store site.

They gathered the horses and sat watching the approaching flames from the west. In the darkness, the fire illuminated the surrounding prairie and low hills. Orange glows dotted the landscape in all directions.

"Kinda pretty, isn't it?"

"Will it really make the grass and berries grow?" Levi asked.

"You bet. In a few weeks, you will see green like you never seen. Like a green blanket draped over the land."

Turon pulled a tobacco pouch from a shirt pocket and rolled a cigarette.

"I remember you called it a green country once," Levi commented.

"It is. The right time of year." Turon lit his cigarette and stuffed the tobacco pouch back into his pocket.

"Ounce wants to run some hounds tomorrow night, if you are game."

"I'll be game. Providing I get those crates unpacked

and put away."

"Ma could spare Ruth to help you."

"I can get by without her if your mother needs help." Levi shifted in the saddle.

"Ma has Lorelei now. She is busting with help. Ruth needs something to keep her busy."

"I should figure a wage to pay Ruth. She helps so much," Levi said with sarcasm.

"Be cheaper to marry her. She wouldn't wear out horses going from the farm to the store." Turon took another drag from the cigarette.

Levi did not respond to that. Turon grinned, letting smoke trail from his nostrils. The orange lines in the night charged into each other in a brilliant display of light. With no more fuel left to feed the flames, the fire died. What light had been so bright from the lively fire was gone. Only the smell of smoke and darkness remained.

Chapter 7

"Wages?" Ruth laughed.

"It's only right. You do so much here."

"You can't afford me. Better save your money for Toe and Lee."

"They will be paid. Worked out trade."

Toe and Lee had helped him swing the new door and set the windows into their frames earlier in the morning. The door and windows needed trimmed out. Levi intended to do just that once he had the store organized. The twins had gone back to the well. Toe filling a bucket with dirt and Lee using a rope to pull the bucket through a block and tackle suspended from a wooden A-frame centered over the hole.

Under the giant oak, the two old Cherokee men watched, speaking to each other in muted tones. Levi stood at the window taking a break from his task and argument with Ruth.

"How old do you think they are?" Levi asked.

"They are twins, so eighteen I think." Ruth arranged glass jars on a shelf.

"Not Toe and Lee. The elders."

"They are old enough they fought in the Battle of Strawberry Moon," Ruth said with pride.

"Battle of Strawberry Moon?"

"In the old days when the first Cherokee came to the western lands, the Osage raided our farms. Kidnapped our women and children. Killed many men. Stole our horses and cattle. We fought back. We waited until the Strawberry Moon. Our men attacked their village. Killed many warriors. Took back our people and livestock." Ruth spoke with pride.

"What year did that happen?" Levi was curious.

"June, eighteen seventeen."

"They would have to be nearly ninety years old," he said.

"Yup, they fought many battles. They don't talk about it." Lowering her voice, she turned to him. "They say they still have the war clubs they used and a chest of Osage scalps."

"Incredible." Levi had a newfound respect for the two men.

"We nearly have everything stocked." Ruth returned to her work.

"I suppose you will head home, then."

"I am home. Least it will be once we are married." Ruth smiled, her eyes mocking Levi, daring him to counter.

"Hello in the store." Turon's voice broke up the battle of wits.

"Yeah," Levi answered.

Turon sat on his bay horse. Cradled in his arm was his Henry rifle.

"Trouble?" Levi searched Turon's eyes for alarm.

"Could be." Turon continued, "Ned Foreman's milk cow is missing.

"Stolen?" Levi asked.

"Maybe. She may be bulling and took off. At any rate, the new baby and the other kids need milk. Maggie has the fever. Old Woman Still is with her. You up for a cow hunt?"

"Yeah, let me grab my hat."

"Maggie need anything?" Ruth looked at her brother.

"Rest for sure. Old Woman Still will see she is taken care of," Turon reassured her. "She's got a poultice for the fever."

Levi emerged from the store carrying his saddle and tack. The revolver stuck in his boot.

"Ruth, can you watch the store?" Levi asked, pausing in front of her.

"Sure, we can discuss my wages when you return." Ruth winked then went inside.

Levi shook his head. Toe and Lee walked up questioning Turon in Cherokee. Levi caught his little strawberry roan mare and saddled her. He led her around for a few moments in a ritual he had developed. She took the weight of the rider more agreeably if she was warmed up. The little mare had a history of bucking for a few rounds if one were to step on her with a cold back.

"Where do we start?" Levi asked, climbing aboard.

"I think she will go to cattle. We ought to split up. Each take one of these hollows to the south. Meet up down where the creek hits the river in Black Fox Hollow. If either one finds her, we will drive her down to that point. Ned's place is there at the river bend. Him and Pa are working the drainages south and west toward Oaks Mission. Ned's kids are scattered from the river to Arkansas."

"Arkansas?" Levi questioned the range.

"Maybe. They are a thirsty lot." Turon turned his horse and drummed his heels, urging it south.

The twins went back to the well. Turon shouted to the old men in Cherokee, and they waved. Levi followed, and the little mare made a few weak crow hops but came up even with Turon's bay.

"Ned's cow is a red roan. She has a jingle bob on her left ear and falling F brand on her left hip," Turon said.

"You think she's with a bull?"

"I'd say she's with a bull or in the market for one," Turon answered. "My bull had some cows hemmed up in this hollow the other day."

"You take that drainage, then, I'll take the one to the east."

"The east is a longer ride. If I don't find anything, I'll circle around and find you." Turon set the bay into a short lope.

Levi eased his mare down the drainage, leaving the prairie. Hardwood timber grew on the hillsides. Burnt patches lay scattered throughout. Levi thought of the berry patches soon to come.

Berries made him think of food, and suddenly he felt hungry. Being hungry, he thought of Ruth's stew then of her.

"Do you think I should just marry Ruth?" Levi leaned forward, patting the roan mare on a shoulder.

Indifferent to his question, the mare continued down the drainage. Levi scanning the ridges for cattle.

"Of course, if I married Ruth, we would have that pinto to contend with."

The mare, still disinterested, continued down the drainage.

"She's not Jewish. Although, I may not be anymore, either."

The mare still ignored Levi's comments.

"I'll never go back to Poland. I could go to New York or Savannah. Find a nice Jewish girl in either of those places."

The mare, as if on cue, passed gas. Her only reply to his monologue.

"Maybe so, but I doubt Ruth would stand for me to

bring a Jewish bride here. She might petition the council and get my license revoked. She would probably kill me. Make the girl a widow."

Levi occasionally stopped and listened for bawling cows, scanning the ridges and the bottom land. Every so often checking his back trail. He soon stopped thinking of hypotheticals and thought of the Foreman family. The kids hungry for milk. The baby and the sick mother.

Ned had bragged about the baby and mother. He was proud and had every right to be proud. He had seen them a few times. All loaded in the farm wagon, coming to his store site. Maggie was an attractive woman. A caring mother. Once again, Levi's thoughts turned to Ruth.

"She has cast an incantation on me. I can't get her out of my head. An old cowboy told me once, talking to your horse is sign a man has spent too much time alone."

Motion caught Levi's eye, and he turned to investigate. Lunging sideways, the mare left him scrambling to stay in the saddle. As quick as she had jumped, she backed up with ears pointed forward. This too caught Levi off guard. Still mounted but his pants caught on the saddle horn, and he was ear to ear with the mare as she kept backing. Her eyes and ears forward.

From a gravel washout, a sow hog grunted almost a bark. A half dozen little pigs gathered around her as she took off running, her tail over her back and ears up.

Levi calmed the mare. Her nostrils flared and ears pitched forward watching the retreating sow and her little ones.

Relieved the mare did not buck, he urged her south down the bottom. The farther he rode, the higher the ridges flanking him rose. He soon came across fresh cow manure. A little hollow to the east had water running out of it and fresh cow tracks and signs of manure going up it.

Levi soon saw calves lounging about and cows grazing. The cows watched as he approached. Some of them with heads up went to their babies. The calves gathered close to their mothers watching Levi and the mare. Thirty cows, Levi estimated. None of them ear marked with a jingle bob or carrying the falling F brand.

On his way down the drainage, he saw two more bunches of cattle. The last one, he found her. A group of twenty cows. A red white-faced bull carrying the Turtle brand following a red roan cow with the left ear marked with a jingle bob. On her left hip, a falling F brand.

"You old hussy. People are out climbing ridges searching for you." Levi tried hazing the cow from the bull.

Busheyhead, as Turon called the bull, was not eager to surrender the cow. He dodged Levi and kept beside the cow.

Levi did not think he had much of a chance of separating the cow from the bull. He drove them both down the creek bottom toward the river and the Foreman farm. The cow was hard to drive, and the bull followed wherever she went. Ignoring Levi, the bull stayed close to the cow.

Levi considered casting a loop around the cow's horns, for she was surely broke to lead, being a milk cow. He did not relish the idea of the little mare breaking into two while dallied to the cow.

The cow stopped, ignoring Levi and his commands to keep moving. The bull came in close behind the cow and stood on his hind legs. The cow bore the weight of him as he did what came naturally. The act in and of itself was short-lived.

Levi considered the amount of work the bull had put into chasing and following the cow. Levi resumed driving the cow toward her home. The bull followed along, keeping a respectable distance from the cow. No longer as interested in being at her side, he took time to graze.

"What you got there?" Turon rode up, surprising Levi.

"A bred milk cow more than likely." Levi reined up, and the cow circled back to join the bull.

"Let me signal we found her." Turon raised his rifle and pointed it in the air firing two spaced shots then suspending it from a string looped on the saddle horn.

"We might as well take them both to the Foreman place. She will come in on her second heat later tonight. She should have a bull handy." Turon loosened his lariat and built a loop.

"I'm sure Ned will appreciate it." Levi maneuvered the little roan mare behind the bull.

"If she has a heifer calf, I'll have to deal Ned out of it." Turon tossed a small loop around the upright horns of the milk cow.

Turon turned his bay toward the cow's home, and the slack rope tightened. She obeyed the rope, following Turon and the bay. Levi eased the bull along behind them.

Near where Black Fox Hollow met the Illinois River stood the log house of Ned Foreman. A horse and mule barn towered over the farmyard on a slight rise. Next to it, a corn crib holding last year's harvest provided shade and shelter to hounds announcing the arrival of Levi and Turon.

Old woman Still stood on the porch watching them approach. When they neared the house, she came to the picket yard fence made of Osage orange branches.

From the house, a toddler wandered out and plopped down on the porch, followed by a girl of three years of age.

"Siyo a-tsu-tsa," she greeted Turon in Cherokee.

Levi understood her when she said, "Hello, boy." The exchange that followed left him confused. He could understand only a little. Picking out a word or two.

Turon listened and nodded. He asked her something about Maggie. Abruptly, she turned away and went into the house. In a moment, she returned and handed him a bucket over the fence. He nodded and rode to the barn, leading the cow.

Levi followed while the bull found some shelled corn in a bucket someone left out.

"It's milking time." Turon climbed down from the bay and led the cow into the barn.

Levi tied the horses to a rail fence then joined the other man in the barn where Turon had placed the milk cow in a headlock. Finding some corn, he dumped it in the cow's trough. She ate as Turon sat on a stool near the cow's udder. His hands held a teat each, and the rhythmic squeeze and tug sent milk streaming into the bucket.

The roan cow flicked her tail, catching him across the face and knocking his hat off.

"Hold her tail, Little Kansas." He furrowed his brow.

"You're pretty good at milking." Levi reached and caught the tip of the cow's tail as she readied for another swat.

"I had plenty of practice. Being the oldest. I thought I gave it up once I ran away to cowboy."

"How are Maggie and the baby doing?"

"Old woman Still said the baby is fine. Maggie is resting, but she will be okay soon enough." Turon kept the rhythm; the milk slowly collecting in the bucket.

A calf bawled from a nearby pen. Hungry for milk.

"Old woman Still said they weaned the calf the other day. Sometimes weaning a calf off its mother will cause the cow to come in heat." Turon continued his rhythm, the sound of the milk filling the bucket changing with the increasing depth. "She smelled the range cows while she was out grazing at night I would bet."

Turon switched to the other two teats and soon had the bucket full. Levi held the tail as Turon gently lifted the bucket. Once clear of the cow, Turon pulled the wooden peg holding the headlock closed. This released the cow, who was now free to go.

"Ma would tear into me if I spilt the milk as a child. Guess the lesson stuck." Turon carefully carried the milk to the log house.

A barn cat lingered around, and Levi assumed he was bumming for a little milk. In Cherokee, Turon told him to go catch a rat. On cue, the cat slinked off. As it did, it drew attention of some hound pups and jumped to the rail fence just in time to avoid the pups.

"Siyo." Ned rode into the barnyard, hailing Turon and Levi.

Close behind was Turon's father John. Ned greeted them with excitement. Turon spoke in Cherokee and motioned to Levi.

Ned slid off the plow horse he had been riding bareback and stepped to Levi, giving him a hard slap on the upper arm then grasping both shoulders. "*Wado*, thank you, Little Kansas." Ned released him as Old Woman Still came out of the house.

Turon handed the bucket to Ned who carried it to the house. One by one, the Foreman children appeared from various directions. All had heard Turon's two gunshots signaling the cow had been found.

Levi retrieved his horse ready to get back to the store.

"Still game to turn some dogs loose tonight?" Turon got his horse as well.

"Might as well. Where do you want to meet?" Levi mounted his mare, awaiting a response.

"I'll swing by and pick you up." Turon turned to see Ned coming out of the house.

Ned strolled to the barn where a half a dozen hound pups were lounging, chewing on bones and hoof trimmings. He reached down and picked up a spotted pup by the scruff of the neck. The pup hung suspended from his loose hide. Ned ran a finger through the pup's teeth inspecting the inside of the mouth. Satisfied with what he saw, he carried the pup to Levi and placed it in Levi's lap.

"He's out of a good stud dog and a better bitch. If he doesn't trail a wolf, I'll kiss your ass on the courthouse square in Tahlequah." Ned stood proud and confident the pup would hunt.

"Are you sure, how much?" Levi was stunned.

"You saved us when you found our cow. Babies need milk. Maggie can't nurse them all. Take the pup." Ned patted Levi's leg.

"Thank you," Levi said, overwhelmed with gratitude as he tucked the pup under his arm.

Riding from the Foreman farm back to the store, Turon remarked most people would trade a sow for a Foreman trail hound. Levi had a new sense of pride. He never had a dog before. Let alone a bona fide trail hound.

CHAPTER 8

Ruth had several customers come to the store while Turon and Levi hunted the Foreman's milk cow. Three wagon loads of families and two lone riders. One being a judge for the Cherokee Nation on his way to the Delaware District courthouse.

She liked working at the store. As a young girl, she had always looked forward to neighbors visiting and church gatherings. She reflected on this as she stood on the porch watching a wagon leave.

"We are going home for the day." Toe slipped a boot off his right foot and dumped a pebble and dirt from it.

"No water?" Ruth asked.

"Not yet. We are sixteen feet down."

"Spare a candy stick?" Lee asked. He stomped his boots and dusted off his clothes.

"I'm sure Levi can afford it." Ruth went into the store and pulled two striped candy sticks from a jar.

"Tell Little Kansas, many thanks." Lee took the candy and handed one to Toe.

They both climbed on a plow horse bareback. Toe reining the old horse and Lee kicking his heels urging home. Ruth watched them for a bit before going back inside. The old Cherokee under the tree moved to the well and inspected Toe and Lee's work.

"Afternoon, miss." A voice startled Ruth as she arranged some bolts of cloth.

"Oh, hello. How can I help you?" Ruth recovered seeing a blue-eyed man standing in the doorway.

"I could use a little tobacco and a few items." The blue-eyed man approached the counter causally checking what items were on the shelves.

"Got any Red Man loose leaf or Cannon Plug?" he asked.

"We have Red Man." Ruth pulled a pouch from a crate under the counter.

"That will do. I see you have some dried peaches. How about a bundle yay big?" The blue-eyed man held his hands cupped together.

"Of course." Ruth scooped the dried peaches onto paper and neatly folded them into an envelope package.

"Quarter pound of cheese." He gestured to a cloth-covered block on the counter.

"Anything else I can help you with?" Ruth pulled the cloth back and retrieved a long well-worn knife.

"Maybe you could, miss. See, my boss is buying steers. He heard there were some white-face stock in the area." The blue-eyed man studied Ruth. "He would pay a bonus for some Hereford cross steers."

Ruth hesitated for a moment. Noise at the door got her attention. The two ancient warriors came inside. The men well in their nineties maneuvered into positions flanking the blue-eyed man.

"Howdy, you two know of any Hereford stock in the area?" the blue-eyed man asked.

The two old Cherokee didn't say anything. Just held blank expressions. The blue-eyed man turned and looked back at Ruth.

"They don't speak English," Ruth said. She wrapped

the cheese and sat it on the counter beside the tobacco and dried peaches.

"Could you ask them for me?"

Ruth spoke in Cherokee asking the old men what they thought of the blue-eyed stranger. One shook his head no. The other spoke softly and briefly.

"They can't help you," Ruth simply said.

"How about you? Do you know of any white-face cattle or a bull in the area?"

She furrowed her brow in thought. She wondered why he asked about a bull. Finally, she answered.

"I don't know of any white-face cattle for sale around here."

This was the truth. Turon had only brought the bull home last fall. It would be August if any white-face calves were born at all.

"That will be seventy cents." Ruth pushed the items across the counter.

"Fair enough." The man laid coins on the counter counting the exact amount.

"Thank you." Ruth collected the coins and laid them in a wooden box Levi had built with dividers for different coins and paper money.

Trace chains rattled outside as a wagon pulled up to the front of the store. Tall climbed from the wagon seat and stepped onto the plank floor of the porch. The boards creaking under his weight.

"Hello, Ruth, Little Kansas about? I brought some curb stones for him. I figure he can use them for the well." Tall blocked the light as he entered through the door.

"Thank you, miss. You have been a great deal of help." The blue-eyed man smiled and gathered his stuff. "Excuse me, big fellow." He moved past Tall and climbed aboard his horse.

Ruth's blood ran cold, and a chill spread from her

lower back up her spine.

"Tall, did you know that man?" she asked with concern.

"Never seen him before. Should I know him?"

"He was asking about white-faced cattle to buy. Asked if I knew who had a Hereford bull."

"Doesn't seem unusual. About time for cow traders to pick up long yearlings."

"He didn't ask you." Ruth moved to window.

"I don't have cattle to sell," Tall replied.

"He doesn't know that. If he really is a cow buyer, he would have asked you."

The old men talked to each other. Tall listened for a moment and went out on the porch watching the rider kick his horse into a short lope.

"As soon as he heard the name Little Kansas, he left in a hurry."

"He wasn't Bill Kirby. I've seen him," Tall said.

"He might know Kirby. Might be working for him." Ruth turned to Tall.

"Where's Little Kansas now?"

"Hunting a milk cow with Turon. Toward the river." She turned south trying to make her brother and Levi materialize.

"I will unload those stones. Then stay with you until Levi or your brother gets back." Tall moved his wagon near the well and started to unload the rocks.

Ruth followed Tall and could no longer see the blue-eyed rider. Like a snake suddenly disappearing into leaves or grass, she worried more now that she couldn't see the rider. Remembering the old men who had moved close to protect her, she turned back to the store. They were gone. Disappeared. She went to the side of the store to see where people usually left horse and mules tied. The two mules the old men rode were gone. Old black mules ancient as the two old warriors.

"Where did those two rascals get off to?" Calm came about her.

She could not imagine what the two old men could have done to the blue-eyed stranger had there been a fight. How brave they must have been when they were young. Still brave, she thought.

The shadow of the giant oak stretched far to the east as Turon and Levi rode up to the store. Ruth came out and stood on the porch.

Tall soon joined her, holding a piece of cheese and chewing another one. "Glad to see you two." He tossed the remaining cheese into his mouth.

"Look who's a houndsman now." Turon motioned to Levi who slid off his mare still carrying the pup.

"He's going to need a guard dog." Ruth's tone was serious and to the point.

Ruth and Tall both explained their concerns and suspicions. How the mention of Little Kansas sent the man on his way and in a hurry. How he asked about a white-face bull.

"We don't know for sure what he wanted. He may have just been a cow buyer. New to the area," Turon said finally.

"Might be. He did seem off a little. Cow traders like to hang out awhile in a place like this. Meet folks. Let themselves be known. He didn't even give his name." Tall stood working a knot out of a shoulder.

The pup lay at Ruth's feet, belly up, soliciting another belly rub.

"What are you going to name the pup?"

"Moses," Levi said while watching the horizon.

"Moses will not do." Ruth scratched the pup's neck.

"Moses is a good name." Levi was defensive.

"He will never learn to spell Moses. Better call him Mo." Ruth leaned close to the pup. "Yes. Mo is what we will call you."

The pup rolled over and sat on his haunches, responding to Ruth's voice.

"He's a wolf hound. A trail dog. You are going to spoil him." Levi furrowed his brow.

"He's a pup." Ruth scratched Mo behind an ear.

"Maybe you should stay at the house for a few nights." Turon was scanning the horizon as he spoke.

"You can't watch me all the time. You have branding to do soon. I've got the revolver." Levi pulled it from his boot and checked the cylinder.

"You're not in this alone. If it was a scout for Kirby, we have the edge." Tall clasped a hand on Levi's shoulder.

"What edge?" Ruth asked.

"Those two old men. Breaking Glass and Wolf. They snuck out and will follow our blue-eyed stranger. Find out where he is headed."

"Tall's right. Those two will find him and let us know. You will come home with us tonight." Ruth was blunt.

"Might as well, Little Kansas. We are running the dogs tonight anyhow." Turon went over to his horse and tightened the cinch.

"Mo, let's go home." Ruth made a squeaky sound with her mouth, and the pup jumped to his feet and followed her to the pinto grazing nearby.

"I've lost my dog." Levi shook his head.

"You can still have a dog, just have to take Ruth in as well." Tall gave Levi a slap on the back and walked to his wagon and team.

Chapter 9

Blue checked several times to see if anyone was following him. He could not see anyone but felt uneasy. He realized they had no reason to suspect anything. The girl had not talked much, Indians seldom did. Just pure luck the big man came in.

He rested and watered his horse at Clouds Creek after crossing Long Prairie. His tracks stuck out across the charred grass of a recent fire. East of the creek, he bypassed the town of Row, a little community, its wooden buildings towering above the surrounding prairie.

He rode east, dropping into a drainage locals called Hog Eye Creek. He avoided Cherokee farmers who stopped to watch him ride through. People had begun to plow little fields in the creek bottom. Wishing to avoid as many people as he could, he turned northeast where two ridges ended in limestone bluffs, creating a funnel in the already-narrow bottom land.

The sun was low, when he stopped briefly at the cast-iron post in the bottom of a hollow. On the west side of the post, *Indian Territory Cherokee Nation* was stamped. On the east side, *The State of Arkansas, United States.*

"Almost home." Blue patted the sweaty neck of the

horse.

He could feel the cool evening air on his damp palm and wiped it on his trouser leg. He urged his horse up a ridge then back down a slope into Coon Creek. Fifty yards from the cabin where he left Kirby, he stopped the horse.

"Hello at the cabin. It's Blue. I'm coming in." Blue listened a moment after he made his announcement for a reply.

The cabin door hung open, but Blue could not see anyone at the door.

Blue dismounted and led his horse the rest of the way to the pole corral. He pulled the saddle and headstall off, turning the horse into the pen without rubbing him down. Blue watched the horse as he trotted to a dirt patch and lay down. Rolling in the dust, dirt clung to its wet hair.

"What did you find out?" Kirby's voice was close, and it spooked Blue.

"Hot spit and monkey vomit, Bill!" Blue caught his breath and eased some. "You shouldn't sneak up on a body that way."

"You should learn to watch your back. Make sure you're recognized before coming into camp." In a calm even voice, Kirby continued, "What did you find out?"

"I found him. Least where he should be."

"Where?"

"There is a new store building where Spring Creek drains off the Long Prairie. An Indian girl was clerking the store, and a big man came in asking for Little Kansas. Said he had some curb stones for his new well in front of the store." Blue carried his saddle and tack to thc porch of tho little cabin.

"An Indian girl?" Kirby was interested.

"A pretty one too. She seemed to oversee the store." Blue lifted a loose floorboard and pulled a jug from a hiding place.

"You didn't see him? The little foreigner?" Kirby studied Blue.

"No. I got the feeling he wasn't far. Didn't see any reason to hang around. Thought I better try to get back here before dark." Blue eased down the cabin wall to a sitting position, pulling the cork from the jug in the same motion.

Kirby walked into the cabin and was there a few minutes before coming back out on the porch.

"As agreed." Kirby dropped one hundred dollars into Blue's lap as he was taking a drink from the jug.

"Dang, Bill, to the point all right." Blue gathered the money and held it to his nose, smelling it.

"I need you to do one more thing for me," Kirby said, looking down at Blue.

"Sure, Bill." Blue tucked the money into a pocket.

"I'm traveling fast once I'm finished with the foreigner. Ride into town in the morning and get me some supplies. Best I'm not seen hereabouts."

"Sure, Bill. Nebo has all a body could ever want. Except a drink, but that's what this is for." Blue handed the jug to Kirby.

"Might take some with me." Kirby accepted the jug and raised it to his lips. He stopped and listened. He heard a sound from the below the cabin. Darkness had settled across the valley. He could still make out the tree line toward the creek.

"What is it?" Blue sat up and stared into the darkness.

"I don't know. Thought I heard something toward the creek."

The two men held their breaths. Neither spoke. As long as Blue could remember, avoiding capture or reaping gains depended on eliminating risk. He listened for horses. He listened for men. A sudden squall and the sound of something moving in the brush put him at ease.

"Raccoons. Raccoons fighting near the creek?" Blue leaned back against the cabin wall.

"Sounds like it."

"You never said what this Little Kansas owes you or did to make you hunt him."

"I'm apt not to either." Kirby handed the jug back to Blue.

"Your business, Bill. Simply curious."

Morning came, and frost shined in the early light. Blue had built a fire in the stove earlier in the night after getting chilled. He now boiled water for coffee. Kirby was not a particularly good host. Although it was sort of Blue's place. A hideout from Molly.

After a lean-and-quick breakfast, Blue rode toward Nebo. He had put to memory what items Kirby wanted. He knew Kirby had a warrant out. For what, he couldn't remember. Didn't matter really. For one hundred dollars, he would more than happily fetch the outlaw groceries.

Thinking of Molly, he decided to stop by the farm. She would be mad at his being gone. Although once he flashed the money in her face, she would calm down soon enough. With the money in mind, he slipped twenty dollars from the bundle and tucked it into his hat band.

"She doesn't need to know how much I've got. Just I got some."

Riding into the farmyard, he saw her before she saw him. She was gathering eggs. Great egg hunt she called it, as her hens ran loose and weren't kept in a coop.

"Good morning, Molly. Pretty as ever." Blue reined up and stepped from the saddle.

Surprised, she jerked upright and arched an eyebrow. "Oh. It's the cattle baron Charlie Goodnight."

She ran a hand through her unkept hair holding it out of her face.

"I got eighty dollars for finding cattle right here." Blue handed her the money.

"Bullshit. What have you really been doing?" She snatched the money from his hand.

"I told you, Molly. Been finding cattle for Bill."

"Bill Howard?" Molly asked.

"Yes. Been all over the Delaware District, even down to the Goingsnake."

"Bullshit. You're a liar, Blue Tate. He said his name was Bill Hawkins." Molly leaned into the punch and caught Blue in the abdomen.

"Molly." Blue coughed and went to his knees, losing his hold on the horse's reins.

"Tell me, what have you really been doing?" Molly's slap landed hard against the side of his head.

"Easy."

"Tell me, Blue." She raised her hand and hesitated.

"Hunting a fellow in the Cherokee Nation, he owes him."

"You in the debt collecting business now Blue? What's he owe him?"

"He didn't say." Blue started getting up.

"Little Kansas his name, or Levi?" Molly stood with her feet apart and hands ready to throw punches.

"How would you know that?" Blue was stunned.

"If you would read the papers instead of using them to wipe yourself, you might learn something." Molly ran to the house and came back with a newspaper in her hand.

"I know a lot of names, Blue. Like Bill Kirby. *Siloam Springs Herald* carries news out of the Nations. Seems your friend was captured last fall by a store clerk called Little Kansas. Your friend Kirby was sentenced to the federal pen in Detroit and was on the way there two weeks ago. He managed to escape in Missouri, along with twelve thousand dollars in cash." Molly had the paper rolled up and swatted Blue with it as she handed it to him.

"Twelve thousand dollars?" Blue looked up from the paper.

"I suppose he could afford the eighty dollars, or was it more? You holding out on me?" Molly raised a hand.

"Quit hitting me." Blue took a quick step back. "Let me think."

"Thinking never was your skill set."

"Molly, please."

"He could have gotten you arrested again. This time, the federals would take you. I ain't got enough hogs to sell to get you off federal charges."

"I haven't done anything illegal."

"That's the problem. You haven't done anything. You haven't been here to plow fields. You haven't been here to mend harnesses. If you aren't going to work this farm or sell enough whiskey to see I'm taken care of, then what good are you to me?"

"What is it you want me to do, Molly?"

"We have as much right to the money as he does. That kind of money, we could go to California, New York, or even London." Molly stood with a hand on a hip, the other pointing at Blue.

"London? I never heard you mention wanting to go to Kentucky."

"Ugh, good thing you are pretty, Blue Tate." Molly looked at the sky and closed her eyes.

"We make a pretty pair," Blue said, taking it as a compliment.

"Where's Bill Kirby now?" Molly spoke slow.

"He's at the Cummings cabin above Coon Creek. Waiting on me. I'm supposed to fetch him some supplies from town."

“Go get his stuff. Stop by here on your way back.”

“He has a carpetbag. He wouldn’t let me touch it. Kept it tucked out of sight,” Blue recalled.

“Must be where he has the money. Go to town. Get what he wanted. Stop back here.” Molly’s face contorted, her brow furrowed and tongue pressing against her cheek.

“What are we going to do?” Blue asked.

“We are going to get rich.” Molly hurried to the house.

Chapter 10

"Coon Creek, they call it. I know the place." Tall held the coffee cup, ready to take a sip.

Glass did the talking between the two old warriors. Wolf kept quiet. Glass told them of following the blue-eyed stranger to the cabin. How they mimicked a raccoon fight so they could slip in close.

"Two men were at the cabin. He said they considered stealing their horses and mule. They had a nice black mule," Tall laughed.

"What do we do?" Levi studied the floor at his feet.

"Goingsnake sheriff doesn't have jurisdiction. We could ride into Siloam Springs. Wire Fort Smith for a marshal." Turon went to the stove and refilled his coffee cup.

"Then what? It would take them forever to get here." Ruth stood with her arms folded across her chest.

"We don't know for sure it was Kirby. Just a man and the blue-eyed man. No law against being blue-eyed." Levi walked to the store window and could see Mo chewing on a stick of wood.

"We could ride over and see for ourselves. If it is Kirby, one of us could ride for the law." Turon sipped his coffee.

"What happens if it is Kirby and he spots us?" Levi asked.

"You kill him," Wolf spoke for the first time and did so in perfect English.

Everyone turned toward the old Cherokee in surprise.

"You speak English?" Levi asked.

"You speak too much. Kill him and be done with it," Wolf said before speaking briefly to Glass in Cherokee. The two left the group and went outside.

"Well, I be. I never knew him to talk English. Had a hint of British accent to it too." Tall took a drink of coffee.

"I don't want to kill Kirby," Levi said flatly.

"Might not have to kill him," Turon smiled. "You caught him once."

"I was lucky, and the deputy marshal just happened to show up."

"You could get lucky again. This time you won't be alone." Turon set his cup on the counter.

"No. You won't." Tall set his cup beside Turon's.

"Ok, then." Levi went to the back room where he had moved his belongings.

From two pegs, Levi took down an old sixteen-gauge shotgun. He slipped the revolver into his boot. In a small canvas sack, he dropped a hand full of shells and cartridges. The sack he stuffed into his coat pocket. From a rack, he pulled his saddle and tack then walked outside to catch the little roan mare.

"What are you going to do?" Ruth had moved up behind Levi as he saddled the little roan mare.

"Find out if Kirby is the other man. If he is, then I'll ride to the wire. Get the marshals." Levi pulled the cinch tight.

"You should take some food. I'll go make up a sack."

"Ruth."

"Yes."

"Maybe you should go home. I can close the store."

"What good will closing the store do?" Ruth's eyes narrowed.

"If we miss him, and he's already headed this way..."

"He'll what, shoot me? He's mad at you. Remember?"

"He could hurt you to get at me."

"I'm just a clerk, aren't I? Did you not offer to pay me wages?"

"You are more than a clerk to me."

"Why, Levi." Ruth smiled, and her eyes brightened. "Is that a proposal?"

"Just because I care about you doesn't mean I'm ready for marriage," Levi blurted out.

"You do care, though, and you aren't just ready for marriage yet. I'll go pack some food for you to take."

He shook his head slowly and led the little mare around to warm her up. He paused near the well.

Tall approached leading his big black horse. "You boys hit water yet?"

"We hit mud." Lee used a stick to get the wet clay from the bucket then drop the bucket back down to Toe.

"If there's mud there's water. Listen, boys. We are going on a hunting trip. See if we can't find Bill Kirby or that blue-eyed fellow."

Toe effortlessly climbed the bucket rope to hear the conversation.

"Can you two stay close? In case Ruth needs help or any strangers show up she can't handle?"

"Yeah, no problem," Lee said.

"Good, we will see you boys later. Can't say for sure when we will be back." Tall mounted his horse.

Turon stepped into the saddle as Ruth came out of the store carrying a canvas sack. She went directly to him.

“See you all don’t get hurt or killed.” Ruth handed the sack to her brother.

“Don’t worry, little sister. It’s just a scouting trip. Let Lorelei know I went for a ride.”

“I will.”

“Choogie or Pa one will be by later to see you get home.” Turon tied the sack to the horn.

“I’ve got the shotgun and I’m capable of riding home alone.” Ruth furrowed her brow.

“I know you are. Any critter or man would lose against you.” Turon grinned.

“Thank you for the victuals, Miss Ruth,” Tall said.

“I’m ready.” Levi rode up.

“Let’s go.” Tall urged his horse out and Turon followed.

Levi hesitated a moment. He stared at Ruth. Her shoulders were back and her gaze matched Levi’s.

“What?” Ruth asked.

“We’ve got some talking to do once I’m back.” Levi buttoned his coat.

“What about?” Ruth knelt to give Mo a scratch behind the ear.

“Wages. We never settled on what I should pay you.”

“Wages?” Ruth’s expression turned to anger as she stood up. “I told you. You can’t afford me.”

“Will you at least watch after our dog?” Levi held the mare back as she was eager to follow the other horses.

“Our dog?” Ruth questioned.

“We can share the dog. Like we can share the store. Minus Turon’s part. He’s part owner.”

“That a proposal?” Ruth arched an eyebrow.

“Do you want it to be?” Levi held the mare steady.

“Yes.”

“Then consider it a proposal.” Levi felt as if his chest would cave in as he said it.

Before Ruth could respond or before he stuck his

foot in his mouth, he let the mare have her head. The little roan was in a short lope as he came even with Turon.

"I'm going to marry your sister," Levi spoke flatly.

"Her idea or yours?" Turon did not act surprised and grinned widely.

"I'm not sure now. Seemed like the only way to keep my dog."

"Hey, Tall. Ruth captured herself a man." Turon raised his voice for the benefit of the big man riding ahead of them.

"About time," Tall said over his shoulder.

The three rode northeast across Long Prairie until it yielded to the trees flanking Clouds Creek. They stopped at a wagon crossing. Tall dismounted and squatted at the water's edge to take a drink.

"What do you remember about the area where the cabin is?" Turon dismounted letting his horse water at the creek.

"A family had the cabin the last time I hauled freight that way. Horse traders is the impression I got from them. I heard folks in Cherokee City say they traded other people's horses. It's kind of a narrow finger of land between the creeks. Slopes gentle like toward Coon Creek. All high bluff toward Spavinaw." Tall stood upright and checked the cinch on his saddle.

"How will we get close enough to see if Kirby is there?" Levi remained in the saddle watching their surroundings.

"Ride up and knock, I recon." Tall mounted the saddle, leather creaking under his weight.

"Kirby knows all of us." Levi considered Tall's idea.

"He may know you two. I know what he looks like, but I doubt he knows me. We never traveled in the same circles. Seen him at a horse race in Tahlequah once. Someone pointed him out before he made off with the cash box at the gate," Tall ran a hand down the back of his shirt and scratched between his shoulders.

"The blue-eyed man saw you at the store," Turon finally spoke.

"If he's there, so be it." Tall examined a tick he pulled off his back. "Little devils are early this year." He flicked the tick into the water.

"We better keep moving." Levi urged the little mare across the creek.

They rode through little bunches of cattle and hogs on the open prairie south of Row. Tall took them east onto Beck Prairie then north across a little valley to a community called Centerpoint. A single-room schoolhouse was in session as they rode by.

"There's a salt lick right over there." Tall stopped on slight rise.

"How far are we?" Turon asked.

"Three miles as a bird flies. There's a hollow down below. May Hollow they call it. We can ride around it and cross the line there." Tall pointed to the northeast. "Short way would be to cross May Hollow and up a steep ridge then back down another hollow."

"Might as well save the horses. In case we need to get somewhere fast later." Turon motioned toward the east and the state line of Arkansas. "Go around?"

"Yeah. If things get sideways over there, Turon, you best beat it west. Get back into the Cherokee Nation. Levi and I are citizens over there. Well, I'm sort of a citizen. You only have to ride a hundred yards to be safe in the Nation."

"We will cross that creek when we come to it." Turon turned to Levi. "You ready?"

"Let's go." Levi started the little roan mare toward the east.

CHAPTER 11

"Sorry, Bill. She figured it out." Blue stood in front of the little porch, eyeing the revolver Kirby had tucked in his belt.

"You shouldn't have brought her here." Kirby watched as the redheaded Molly climbed off a red mule, grunting in her effort.

"Neither of you *gentlemen* would help a lady off her mule?"

"Here, Molly." Blue moved to her offering a hand after the fact.

"Put the animals away, Blue." She slapped his hand from her and marched to the porch where Kirby still stood.

Blue took his horse and the red mule to the pole corral.

"You're a famous man," She said.

Kirby said nothing.

"Papers tell your description good. Even got a reward out for you because you broke that marshal up some."

"He didn't die?" Kirby asked.

"No. He's alive. You wouldn't have much attention except you took the railroad's money. Those railroads take that behavior personal."

"What money?" Kirby asked.

"The twelve thousand you helped yourself to before you hopped off the train."

Molly took a step closer.

"Wasn't no twelve thousand dollars," he said flatly.

"Maybe not. But it must have been a sizable amount. Cause they are searching for you. Searching everywhere." Molly grinned.

"How much do you weigh?" Kirby's eyes narrowed.

"What?"

"I was wondering what you weighed. Not sure if it would be easier to throw you off that bluff or stuff you under the floorboards."

"You need us." Molly grinned.

"Why do I need you two?"

"You have been lucky." Molly took a step onto the porch. "Word is out on you. Anywhere you go, you will stick out like a blister. That scar makes you a marked man, worse than banished Cain."

"The federals and railroad detectives won't be hunting for two men and a woman. Brother."

Molly was now within arm's reach of Kirby, her voice lowered.

"Brother?"

"You see, sir. My husband and I are accompanying my brother west to meet his family." Molly grinned. "Yes, ma'am, he's my brother. Him and my husband are partnering on a ranch. See how easy it is."

Blue moved to the cabin slowly. He had removed his hat then placed it on his head. He now examined a button on his coat hanging by loose thread.

"Blue." Kirby raised his voice.

Blue stepped onto the porch.

"Yeah, Bill?" He must not have seen the fist in time to react.

Molly seen it and heard it. Kirby's fist landed hard on Blue's jawline. Blue fell limp off the porch landing in the dust. The blow took him out, and he immediately started snoring.

Molly's heart rate quickened. She felt warm and her jaw loosened. Her previous rigid expression went slack, and she raked her tongue across her lips.

"You know I am right." She recomposed herself, but her voice was breathy.

"What do you want?"

"I'm not greedy. Just two thousand dollars and a ticket to San Francisco."

"Just one ticket?"

"Better make it two tickets." Molly glanced down at Blue moving slowly.

"What the hell, Bill?" Blue coughed and rolled over, working his jaw.

"I asked you to bring me groceries. Not a travel guide."

"I told you she was smart, Bill." Blue regained his feet.

"She's a real catch." Kirby's sarcasm lost on Blue.

Molly grinned. The sarcasm not lost on her. She continued to grin knowing the hook had been set.

"What's this business with the store clerk? He got gold stashed away?" Molly asked.

"If he does, I don't know about it," Kirby snapped.

"So, this is just for revenge because he got the drop on you last fall?" she asked, moving closer to Kirby.

"Those papers seem to have a lot of information." He took a step back upwind from her.

"They do." Molly moved closer to Kirby. "A person just doesn't open a store unless he has the capital to do so."

"You said they had a red white-faced bull, Bill." Blue joined the conversation. "Those don't come cheap."

“He might have money. I don’t know.” Kirby edged away from Molly.

“He must have something worth taking if you are willing to spend eighty dollars on Blue to go scout for you.” Molly searched for a reaction.

Kirby gave Blue a sidelong look.

“You blue-eyed bastard.” Molly turned on Blue who stepped back out of arm’s reach. “You were holding out on me.”

“What’s your plan to get out of this country?” Kirby changed the subject.

“We ride to Baxter Springs, Kansas. Catch the train there to Kanas City. From there, on to California.”

“You make it sound easy,” Kirby said.

“It is easy. You men are the ones who complicate things. Like revenge on some store clerk.”

“He’s my business.” Kirby raised his voice.

“He’s our business if you get shot or captured. Whatever you are going to do, do it today. Tomorrow, we need to make tracks for Baxter. Take Blue.” Molly matched Kirby’s irritation.

“I don’t need Blue.”

“I need Blue. To protect my interest. Either him or I are going to always be with you. Until we get you delivered out of this part of the world. We are your only chance of getting out of here.” Molly grinned. “You done lingered too long.”.

“You have to admit, Bill. She makes sense.” Blue once again tried to contribute to the conversation.

Kirby took a step toward Blue.

“Hold on, Bill. Please.” Blue took several steps back.

“One thousand. You can buy your own ticket.” Kirby turned to the grinning Molly.

“Fifteen hundred or you can dodge the Pinkerton men and marshals on your own.” Molly stood firm staring down Kirby.

"Blue. Saddle the horses." Kirby still eyed Molly.

"Sure, Bill." Blue retrieved Kirby's saddle from the shed and caught his horse.

"Excuse me." Kirby went into the cabin.

Molly watched him through the open door. He rolled the carpetbag and tucked it under his arm. From a nail, he retrieved his hat and was back on the porch. Blue was in the pole pen getting Kirby's horse ready.

"That the money in the carpetbag?" Molly had taken a seat on an upturned wash tub.

"What if it is?" Kirby's eyes narrowed.

"You made a wise decision. You stand a better chance with me than you do alone." Molly smiled.

"What about Blue? He is going with us?" Kirby lifted a loose floorboard with the toe of his boot.

"He goes with me." Molly was curious about the loose floorboard.

"Then here's to us getting out of the territory." Kirby pulled a crock jug from the space under the porch.

Molly watched him take a drink and sat the jug back into its spot. Kirby sat the board back in place and walked to the corral. Blue handed him the reins to his horse and went to the porch.

"You're a smart one, Molly." Blue grinned at Molly sitting on the wash tub like it was a throne.

"Stay with him. Don't let him out of your sight." Molly motioned toward Kirby.

Molly watched as the two men rode down the slope toward Coon Creek and the state line. As their horses splashed across the creek, she was lifting the porch floorboard. A moment later, she drank from the jug. The smooth clear liquid was warm in her throat. The hue in her cheeks matched her hair by the time the riders topped the next ridge.

"Fifteen hundred my ass. I'll get it all." She took another drink.

Chapter 12

"I see a couple of mules in the pen. No horses," Levi said.

"There are two sets of tracks coming out of the creek. They are recent." Turon motioned to the creek bank.

"I hear something." Tall had his head turned, his better ear toward the sound.

"I hear it too. It's coming from the cabin." Levi cocked his head around. "It's singing."

The three listened and Tall recognized it. Soon it became clear. A woman's voice loud.

"And first he sent letters, and then he sent none,

And three times into prison, I dreamt he was thrown;

So I shore my long tresses, and stained my face brown,

And went for a sailor from Limerick town."

"I'm going to ride in." Tall mounted his big horse.

"Be careful." Turon pulled his rifle up and checked the action.

Tall crossed the creek and rode up the slope. The woman's voice became clearer.

"With that to King William himself I was brought,

And his mercy for Desmond with tears I besought

He considered my story, then smiling, said he
The young Irish rebel for your sake is free."

He rode up close to the cabin. The woman sat on the porch. In her hand was a jug and she was singing. Her eyes closed. She stopped singing and chuckled to herself.

"Fine voice you have, ma'am."

"You're a big son of a bitch." Molly squinted at Tall.

"I'm wanting to buy horses. I heard you sold horses," Tall lied.

"They're gone. Gone to Texas." Molly pointed to the letters G T T carved into the door.

"I see." Tall hesitated, thinking of what to say next.

"We ain't got no horses for sale." Molly stood up.

"There's a blue-eyed fellow that stays here. Is he about?"

"He rode off with—" Molly caught herself. "You the law, you big bastard?"

"No, I tend to avoid the law. You say he rode off with someone?"

"What do you want?" Molly was suspicious even in her careless state.

"Horses if they be for sale."

"We ain't got no horses." Molly was hateful.

"Well, you have a good day, ma'am." Tall turned his horse down the slope.

"Hillbilly bastard, horses."

Tall heard her talking to herself as he rode to where Turon and Levi waited.

"She's alone, I think. Caught her by surprise. She's also higher than a kite. Had a jug of untaxed liquor."

"How about Kirby or the blue-eyed stranger?" Levi asked.

"She slipped up. Said the blue-eyed man rode off with someone. Then she caught herself. Became unfriendly."

"Could be their tracks crossing the creek." Turon

motioned at the creek bank.

"We don't know for sure where they gone." Tall looked over his shoulder toward the cabin." We don't even know for sure who they are."

"Do we still wire the marshals?" Levi asked.

"What would we say? Blue-eyed man buying cattle, stop." Turon shook his head.

"I think we should get back to the store. If it was Kirby, he's gone now." Levi mounted his horse.

"We all know what Kirby looks like. One of us could camp out on the ridge. Keep an eye out on him." Tall motioned to the high ridge behind the cabin.

"Take a little bit to get around unnoticed." Turon studied the lay of the land.

"I've got all afternoon." Tall stuck a finger in his ear, removing some wax and wiped it on his leg.

"How long will you stay?" Levi asked.

"Till they get back and I can see who they are. The little mule is a pack mule. I doubt they left for good. Also, their woman is still there."

"Here, take this." Turon handed Tall the sack of food Ruth had thrown together.

"If you see him, Kirby that is, slip away and get the law. He's mean." Levi held the mare steady.

"I can be mean myself, Little Kansas. But don't worry. I'll slip away."

"Maybe I should stay with you." Turon studied the ridge line.

"You two go back. We don't know for sure where they went or who they even are." Tall drummed his heels and moved his big horse up the west bank of Coon Creek.

"Watch yourself, Tall." Turon turned his horse and urged him west with Levi following.

"I don't like it," Levi said. Where do you think they went?"

"If it is their tracks, they are headed the same way we are."

"That's what I'm afraid of." Levi drummed his heels into the mare's sides.

Both Turon's and Levi's horses were grain fed and accustomed to travel. They short loped until both Levi and Turon worried about taxing the willing animals and walked them for a half mile before urging them into another short lope.

They took the most direct route they could. Up a long slope to a high ridge, they passed under virgin timber. Giant oaks, hickory, and the occasional pine grove blocked out the sun. The lowest limbs hung ten feet above horse and rider. They met no obstructions until they descended the ridge Tall had mentioned. Steep, it fell away to the hollow below. Turon let his bay have her head and reached back at one point grabbing her tail to prevent tumbling over her head.

The little mare Levi rode picked her way down the slope. Loose rocks sliding under her, she kept her footing. They let the horses rest briefly at a spring branch in the bottom of the hollow.

"I see why Tall was eager to go around." Turon tightened his cinch.

"There must be a better way down." Levi flipped the split reins around the mare's neck and mounted.

They rode on past the Centerpoint schoolhouse and down a creek bottom until it turned north. From there, they rode up a hollow and onto the Beck prairie. Neither spoke as they continued. The occasional cow with calf trotted away from the riders. Once, a herd of hogs leaped from a persimmon grove and scattered. The little mare of Levi's eyeing the swine.

"It will be dark by the time we get there." Levi finally broke the silence.

"We will go to the store first." Turon scanned the

horizon.

Tall sat with his back to a shag bark hickory. He could see the cabin below just beyond the tree line. He had worked around the ridge and left his horse tied a couple of hundred yards away. Far enough he worried about him, but he dared not have him closer. If the men rode mares, the scent of the big horse could cause them to nicker, giving away his position.

"Lead with the geldings, the captain would say," Tall whispered to himself.

The redheaded Molly moved about the cabin yard talking and singing to herself. Occasionally taking a drink from the crock jug, she kept close. Tall could make out some of the songs. Irish mostly except for a haunting rendition of "Barbara Allen." It reminded Tall of his own mother singing to him when he was a child in Tennessee.

"When he was dead and laid in grave, her heart was struck with sorrow. O' mother, mother, make my bed. For I shall die tomorrow." He spoke the words softly as to a sleepy baby.

A fox squirrel caught by surprise as the big man scratched the back of his head, jumped to attention. He stood still, waiting for the big man to move again. When Tall refused to move, the squirrel turned his head away from Tall then jerked it back trying to catch him in movement.

The squirrel eventually went back to his work searching under leaves for his autumn stashes. Tall did move but only a little. This sent the squirrel scrambling up a red oak tree. His bark of alarm echoed on the ridge side. He moved about the tree refusing to be a sitting target and constantly barking his alarm.

"Easy, little feller. I'm no danger," Tall whispered.

The squirrel continued his call of alarm.

Below, he could see the redheaded woman gathering firewood. Once, she stopped and squatted, causing him to avert his eyes momentarily before she went into the cabin. The squirrel soon accepted Tall's presence and stopped his barking.

"No woodsman is she, or Cherokee. The squirrel would have sent her to search the ridge or taking cover." Tall adjusted his seat.

The sun was low, and the ridge had the valley in shadow. Smoke soon drifted from the stove pipe in the cabin roof. What breeze there was drifted down the ridge and carried the smoke with it.

"Bet she's cooking or about to cook." Tall's stomach rumbled at the thought.

Remembering the sack, he opened it and pulled out a piece of cheese.

"Cold camp tonight." He watched the western sky turning the color of various fruits. "Hope them boys make out all right." He heard the cabin door swing open.

The redheaded woman went to the pole corral and caught the red mule. She led the mule to the creek to let him water. She returned the red mule to the corral and attempted to close the gate as the black mule tried to pass through.

"You're not my responsibility." The redheaded woman waved her arms and hazed the little black mule back into the corral.

"At least water him," Tall whispered.

He watched as she trotted toward the cabin. Stopping halfway, she turned back to the corral. She stood with hands on her hips and a minute passed.

"Just because that son of a bitch Kirby forgot about you doesn't mean you should suffer." She stomped back to the corral and led the little black mule to water.

"Kirby." Tall's blood ran cold.

He weighed his options. He could wait and just shoot the outlaw like Old Man Wolf suggested. Less trouble for everyone involved. As much as Tall liked to avoid the law, he knew what he needed to do.

"Orchard City is the nearest wire office." Tall stood and slowly worked his way up the ridge to his horse in the fading light.

Chapter 13

"It's not a cigarette, Choogie." Ruth swept the floor in front of the counter, working her way to the door with Mo growling at the broom.

"Sure it is, Ruthie." The boy Choogie held a peppermint stick like a cigarette and mimicked flicking ash off onto the floor.

"Why are you even here?" Ruth humored the boy making a show of sweeping the imaginary ash.

"Told you, Pa wanted me to see you got home all right. He went down to the river to help Ned with a wheel hub."

"I feel safer knowing you are around."

"Pa was killing bears at my age." Choogie realizing his sister's sarcasm.

"We got water, Miss Ruth." Lee ran into the store excited. "Sweet water, taste good," He said.

Ruth and Choogie followed Lee out to the well. The old men, Glass and Wolf, stood looking down into the hole. In the bottom of the hole, Toe had water pooling at his feet and rising.

"How deep is the well, Toe?" Ruth shouted down the hole.

"This rope is thirty feet long. There's five or six feet

of slack on the end of it." Toe leaped up grabbing the rope, climbing up hand over hand.

In Cherokee, Glass spoke softly, "Twenty-four."

"Just need to curb it up now. Maybe build a cover." Lee was proud of their work.

"Wells have names. We will have to name this one Hogshooter or the Toelee well."

"I like Toelee." Choogie sucked on his peppermint stick.

"You all did a good job." Ruth turned to the east and the vacant prairie as if expecting to see riders.

"We can ride home with you, Ruth." Lee offering escort.

"Choogie is here. He can escort me to the house. You two should head home. I'm going to close the store since it's late." Ruth turned west at the sun settling into a bath of orange and red.

"We don't mind," Toe seconding the offer of escort.

"We will be fine."

"Well. We will stay until you are on your way," Lee finally said.

The old men caught their mules and rode off toward the north to Dry Creek where their families farmed. Choogie was sitting on a mule and holding Ruth's pinto gelding as she closed the door of the store.

"Here, soldier. You can carry the shotgun." Ruth handed the shotgun to her brother as she took the reins of the pinto with Mo under her other arm.

"We will be back tomorrow and start curbing up the well." Lee jumped on behind Toe on their old plow horse.

"Little Kansas will be happy with you two." Ruth watched as the two beamed with pride and rode toward their home.

"Eddy?" Choogie turned to her with the peppermint sticking out of his mouth.

"What?"

"Ready?" He removed the candy stick from his mouth.

"Lead on." Ruth followed Choogie and his mule into the twilight.

Riding down the trail along the creek, the trees made an already-darkening day darker. Ruth never minded the darkness or what lived in the night. An owl sounded his night call in an almost-human voice. "Who cooks for you, who cooks for you all."

"Ruthie?" Choogie halted his mule.

"It's okay, Choogie." Ruth rode up even with the boy.

"Ruthie?" He motioned in front of them.

A rider appeared from the shadow of an Osage orange tree. Choogie brought the shotgun to level at the rider. Before Ruth could say or move, a man materialized from the darkness.

A dreadful sound made Ruth's heart jump as a gun barrel smacked the side of Choogie's head.

"Choogie!" Ruth cried out, reaching for the falling boy.

She managed to slow his fall as he slipped from her between the mule and pinto, crumpling to the ground. The mule stood still, and the pinto pranced aside. Soon Ruth was on the ground scrambling to reach the shotgun. The pup running for cover.

Finding it, her right hand grasped the grip and trigger guard. A heavy boot came down hard on her hand. She barely had time to register pain when the back of a hand struck the side of her face knocking her back.

"Stay put, ma'am. He's a boy, Bill. Indian boy." Blue nudged the limp body of Choogie with the same boot he had smashed Ruth's hand.

"Where's the man they call Little Kansas?" Kirby asked as he climbed off his horse.

"He's just a boy, Bill," Blue interrupted. "I hit him hard."

"Shut up, Blue. He was man enough to point a shotgun at me."

"Where's the man they call Little Kansas?" Kirby yanked Ruth from the ground and held her close. "You understand American?"

"He's gone." Ruth's fist doubled and landed hard against Kirby's left eye socket.

A flash of pain and white light overcame Kirby's left eye. In his rage, he struck Ruth, sending her to the ground. She rolled away and was back on her feet ready to attack him again.

She heard the hammer cock on the revolver. She could see in the fading light the shape of it thrust in her direction. Mo growled some distance away.

"You stay there and be still, or I'll have him cave in the rest of this boy's head." Kirby's empty hand motioned to Choogie.

Ruth turned to see the man called Blue pick Choogie up from the trail and sit him up against the base of a sycamore tree. The pup who had run from the scramble now licked Choogie.

"He's alive. Just had his bell rung," Blue reassured her and scratched the pup behind the ears.

"Thought I told you to shut up?"

Kirby turned back to Ruth.

"Where's the man they call Little Kansas?"

"He's out looking for you." Ruth was calm and collected.

"Me?" Kirby didn't believe her.

"You are Bill Kirby, are you not?"

"I am."

"I'm Blue Tate." Blue introduced himself as if he were at a picnic social.

"Blue, shut up and get the horses," Kirby demanded.

Blue hung his head and got the horses. The mule still stood by close.

"Who are you to him?" Kirby turned his attention back to Ruth.

"Who?"

"Little Kansas." Kirby raised his voice.

"I just work for wages." Ruth straightened her dress.

"I bet. He was traveling with an Indian girl, but you ain't her. You appear full blood. She had a more high-class yellow look about her."

"I wouldn't know." Ruth folded her arms.

"He was also traveling with a full-blood Cherokee. Turtle was his name."

Ruth remained silent but her eyes darted away from Kirby's gaze.

"I bet you are a sister. I bet Little Kansas would come a running if he knew I had you."

"I told you." Ruth spoke harshly. "I work for wages."

"What's your name?"

"Ruth."

"Blue. Leave the boy, mule, and the pup. Get her mounted on the pinto Indian pony." Kirby went to his horse and climbed on.

"Ma'am, you heard him." Blue led the pinto close by so she could mount.

"Would you help me?" Ruth appeared sweet.

"Blue, stay out of arm's reach of her. She damn near took out my eye."

Blue hopped back, accustomed to an abusive woman.

"Are you sure he's all right?" Ruth asked Blue about Choogie.

"Yes, ma'am. I've been hit as hard, and I've turned out fine."

This did not comfort her. As they rode away, the pup by Choogie's side barked but did not abandon the boy.

Soon they were at the store.

"Stay on the horses. If she moves, kill her." Kirby dismounted and walked to the door of the darkened store.

"You shopping, Bill?" Blue pointed his rifle at Ruth.

"Shut up." Kirby turned the knob, and it gave way, yielding to his shoulder as he pushed.

"What's he doing?" Ruth turned to Blue.

"I don't know." Blue held his rifle on Ruth as ordered.

Through the windows, a glow from a match could be seen. Ruth feared the outlaw Bill Kirby could be preparing to torch the store. She was relieved when he came to the door and blew out a match. In the darkness, she could make out him lodging something in the door.

"This will go easier on you if you just do what we say." Kirby climbed on his horse.

"What are you going to do?" Ruth sat on the pinto, her weight on her toes ready to kick the horse into a run.

"First, we are going to tie your hands and put a lead line on your horse. Second, we are taking a little trip." Kirby tossed some rope to Blue.

"Where are we going?" she demanded.

"You'll see soon enough. Blue, make those knots neat. Tie her hands behind her back."

Ruth wanted to cry and wince as Blue bound her hands together. She didn't. She got mad. She stared at Kirby with contempt.

"If you turn me loose and leave, you may survive." Ruth did not beg; she made a matter-of-fact offer to the two men.

"You do as told, and you may survive," Kirby countered.

"Ma'am, hope that isn't too uncomfortable." Blue

tugged at the rope, setting the knots.

"Blue, she would have killed both of us earlier if you hadn't taken the shotgun from her."

"I know, Bill. She's still a lady. Indian but still a lady."

"Mount up, Blue. Let's get back to the cabin." Kirby drummed his heels and led the way into the darkness.

Low in the east, the moon started to rise. Providing some light to the riders.

Ruth thought she saw two riders for a moment in the distance but wasn't sure. She knew Turon and Levi were out there somewhere. She prayed for Choogie to be well. She rode with her toes in the stirrups. Her hands bound behind her, she focused on staying in the saddle. She considered jumping from the horse and running to the brush, but Blue had tied a rope around her waist.

Into the night, they rode. Kirby leading the way followed by Blue who constantly turned to her. As hard as he had been to Choogie, he took care to see she was safe. Apologizing several times for the treatment until Kirby silenced him.

She recognized the area they traveled. Only until they passed close by Row could she not name the family farms they rode by. She was tired, although her anger persisted and fueled her stamina. If she could only get her hands free, she would make a break. If she could not get away, she would take another jab at Kirby's good eye.

Chapter 14

"Hear that?" Levi reined up the little mare, turning his head trying to pick up the sound.

Turon did not comment. He stopped his bay.

"Horses maybe." Levi stared into the direction where he heard the sound. He closed his eyes, trying to amplify his hearing.

"Maybe. I didn't hear anything," Turon finally said.

"Probably nothing." Levi set the little mare on her way.

They were less than a mile from the store. The charred ground they covered made an endless void in the night. As they approached the store, Levi could make out the building in the light of the rising moon.

"Ruth closed up shop." Turon reined up at the porch.

"Yeah. I hope she's home by now." Levi dismounted.

"We should get home ourselves."

"Where's Mo?" Levi bounded up on the porch.

"I bet she took the pup home. It's hers now anyway."

Levi went to the door and grabbed the knob. As he opened it, he heard something fall to the floor and his boot caught it in the doorway. He bent over and picked up a piece of folded paper, the kind he wrapped items in for customers.

"What is it?" Turon asked.

"A note. I think." Levi carried the paper inside.

Walking to the counter in the dark, he reached for the little tin of matches he kept on there. He found them knocked over. Several scattered on the wood plank.

"Need a light?" Turon entered the store behind Levi, his Henry rifle at the ready.

"I got a match here. Ruth must have left in a hurry. She's doesn't usually leave a mess like this." Levi struck a match and lit a kerosene lamp.

Holding the lamp in one hand, he unfolded the note with the other and laid it on the counter. His pulse quickened and a rush of fear raced through him as he read the note.

"Little Kansas, we have Ruth. Come alone and bring one thousand dollars to cabin where Coon Creek and Spavinaw come together by noon tomorrow. Bring law and she dies. Bring help and she dies. Bill Kirby."

"What's it say?" Turon moved closer so he could see the note.

"Here." Levi pushed the note toward Turon and placed the lamp on the counter.

"We can get the money." Turon laid the note on the counter beside the light.

"He doesn't want the money. He wants me to be there alone."

"First, we need fresh horses. Let's go to the house. Second, we are getting help. You aren't going in there alone." Turon turned and ran out the door, spooking the horses.

Levi blew the lamp out and was right behind Turon. He jumped from the porch onto the little mare. She didn't offer any objection and moved out quickly following Turon and the bay down the trail toward the Turtle Farm.

As they approached the timber along the creek, they both heard the bark of a pup. In the darkness, they could make out a dark shape in the trail.

“Mo.” Levi rode up even with Turon.

“Yeah, and it’s Choogie’s mule.” Turon stopped and dismounted.

“Turon,” a weak voice called out from the shadows.

“Choogie?”

“Turon. I don’t feel good.” Choogie was sitting up with his head cradled in his hands.

“What happened here?” Turon knelt and the pup Mo was immediately on Turon, licking him and darting between him and Choogie.

“Ruthie and I were riding home. A man rode out from behind a tree. Someone hit me, I think. I just woke up.”

“When did this happen? Before or after sundown?” Turon felt the swelling lump on the boy’s head.

“After.” Choogie used a weak hand to keep the pup Mo from climbing on him.

The sound of Choogie’s saddle hitting the ground caught Turon’s attention.

“What are you doing?” Turon stood up and faced Levi.

“Taking this mule.” Levi had loosened the cinch and swung his saddle and blanket from the mare onto Choogie’s mule.

“Taking it and doing what?” Turon moved close to confront Levi.

“You need to get Choogie home. He may need a doctor or Old Woman Still. I’m going to get Ruth.” Levi pulled the cinch tight.

“We can go together.”

“Get Choogie home. Then get help.” Levi swung into the saddle and leaned over and caught the reins of the little mustang mare.

"Just wait, don't go alone." Turon jumped aside avoiding the mare as Levi urged the mule into the darkness leading the mare now riderless.

Turon stood in the trail. His brother in need of help. His sister kidnapped. His friend rode off into the unknown.

"Let's get you home, Choogie." Turon picked up the boy and slid him into the saddle.

"Come on, Mo. Let's go home." The pup lingered then followed Turon who had climbed up behind Choogie, holding him in the saddle.

"Where's Ruthie?" Choogie asked.

"Little Kansas is going to get her." Turon guided his horse home as he held Choogie.

Levi was thankful for the easy gait of the mule compared to the little mare. Now, he knew the sound he heard had been Kirby and Ruth. They had three or four miles on him. Depending on how fast they traveled, he could overtake them in the darkness.

What dim light from the moon helped illuminate his way. He could make out the trees along Clouds Creek when he stopped to let the mare drink. The mule declined the water. He could not remember how old Choogie's mule was. He brought the mare in case he needed to swap out mounts. Although the mare had traveled all day, she was hardy. He had not pushed her past her abilities. As cold backed as she was, she had heart. With her burden of saddle and rider removed, she was recovering well.

He did not wish to tax the mule as he crossed the Beck Prairie and let the mule travel in his natural gait. His eyes scanned his surroundings. He once thought he saw the markings of Ruth's pinto, but it turned out to be a spotted cow. Its bell clanging as it ran from his path.

"Tall will be there." He rode through the night.

Chapter 15

"State your business," a voice from the wood plank sidewalk demanded.

"I need to wire the federal marshals." Tall reined up and answered the voice.

"I'm the night watchman." The voice came from a middle-aged man appearing from the darkness.

"Who can I get to send a wire?" Tall turned at the night watchman.

"Telegraph operator. He's in bed like any good citizen should be at this hour."

"Go wake him."

"What's so emergent it can't wait until morning?"

"What business is it of yours?" Tall replied.

"I'm the night watchman."

"We ain't dealing with a peeping Tom or town kids tipping outhouses." Tall raised his voice at the watchman. "Bill Kirby is nearby and if someone doesn't act fast, he will slip away."

"The fellow who escaped the train a few weeks ago? There's a reward out on him." The watchman rubbed the stubble on his chin, ignoring the urgency in Tall's voice.

"Howard can get a wire out. If there's anyone down

the line to receive it. Nelson's a sworn deputy. We better get him."

"Fetch Howard so we can get a wire out."

"He's newly married to one of those Barnett girls. He might not be eager to get out of bed."

"Fetch him."

"All right. He won't be happy, but I'll wake him up." The watchman sauntered down the street.

"No need to rush," Tall said sarcastically and followed the watchman down the dirt street.

"Big fellow, I get paid by the same whether I walk or run."

"Must pay well."

"Doesn't pay much at all. If I ran everywhere, I run the risk of falling. If I fall, I could get hurt. Might need doctoring. Doctoring cost money." The watchman continued his slow pace.

"You could do something else."

"I picked apples and peaches for a while. Wasp makes me swell up too much. Run the risk of choking on my tongue."

"You sound like a careful man." Tall continued to ride his big horse, following the watchman.

"I am what some people call risk adverse." The watchman continued his pace down the street.

"That some kind of ailment?"

"Means I'm calculated. I don't make a move unless I'm sure the outcome." The watchman glanced over his shoulder at Tall.

"Night watchman job could be dangerous." Tall glanced down at the man.

"Could be in some places. Orchard City not so much. Now if they bring the railroad here, then it will change things. More people, the higher the risk of bad actors."

"Might force a career change for you." Tall followed the man around a corner.

"I've pondered it. Although, more people would mean more money in the town's budget for a night watchman." The watchman paused at a yard gate.

"This is Howard's place." He opened the gate and walked down the path to the porch.

"More money more problems." Tall dismounted and slipped the reins over a picket in the yard fence.

"Now that's a problem I haven't been plagued by. Hello in the house. Howard, we got a man here needing to send a wire message." He rapped on the door.

"Who is it?" a voice from the house asked.

"It's me, Derrell."

Tall could see through a window a lamp lighted and a glow coming to the door. It opened and a man appeared in the doorway holding the lamp.

"He needs a wire at this hour?" Howard stood in a nightgown barefoot with a sleeping cap sat back on his head.

"What's wrong, Howard?" A woman's voice came from the darkness.

"Derrell has a man here that needs to make a wire is all." Howard spoke into the darkness then turned back to Derrell.

"I hate to disturb you, but I need to get a wire to the U.S. marshal's office in Fort Smith." Tall had moved down the path and stood at the front step, his height towering over Derrell the night watchman.

"Why yes. Yes, sir." Howard's voice cracked upon Tall's sudden appearance. "Are you with the marshal service?"

"No, but I have information that will not wait till morning."

"Of course. I will try. Give me a minute to put on clothes."

Howard closed the door, and Tall heard a woman's voice asking questions. Derrell stepped off the porch and Tall followed him out of the yard.

"We should get Nelson if it's almighty important." Derrell the watchman crossed his arms against the night chill.

"Go get him, then." Tall picked up his horse's reins.

"His place is on the way. It's the white house behind the store."

"What is the message?" Howard closed the gate and buttoned his coat.

"Bill Kirby in cabin on border of Benton County and Cherokee Nation where Coon Creek and Spavinaw come together." Tall tried to not waste words.

"Bill Kirby. Cabin. Benton County. Coon and Spavinaw Creek X. It will be a dollar that way, two dollars your way." Howard finished counting the words on his fingers.

"Get to it, Mister Howard." Tall pulled a dollar coin from a pocket and held it out.

"Yes, sir, right away."

"There's a reward out on Kirby. Read it in the paper last week," Derrell remarked as if Howard hadn't read the same paper.

"You should tell Nelson. If you haven't already." Howard started toward the telegraph office.

"Going to do it now." Derrell moved at a pace slower than the telegraph operator down the street.

Tall was ready to leave. He felt his work was done. It would be up to the marshals and Benton County now. Although, he felt he should at least tell the deputy in person. He didn't have much faith in the risk adverse watchman. Howard continued to the telegraph office, and Tall and Derrell stood before a white house behind a store.

"Who goes there?" a deep voice rumbled from the darkness.

"It's me Derrell. Got a man here with information

you may find interesting."

Tall noticed deputy Nelson did not light a lamp. He stayed in the darkness. When the door did open, Tall could tell the deputy stood to the side of the doorway, letting the door swing open, his body behind the wall. Only after Tall felt he had been well inspected did deputy Nelson step outside with revolver in hand.

"What's a matter, Derrell?" Nelson eyed the big man. "Who you got with you?"

"I'm Tall Maul. Live over in the Nations."

"You haul freight about." Nelson studied the big man.

"Yes, sir."

"What information do you have for me, Mr. Maul?"

"He's found Wild Bill Kirby," Derrell interrupted.

"Derrell, you better get back to your duties. Mr. Maul, come on inside." Nelson moved aside motioning for Tall to come into the house.

Derrell lowered his head and shuffled back toward Main Street. Nelson lit a match and soon had a kerosene lamp glowing. A woman appeared in a doorway with a shotgun cradled in her arms.

"Deputy business, Carrie. You go on back to bed." Nelson opened the stove door and placed a chunk of wood on orange coals.

"Ma'am." Tall removed his slouch hat.

"Tell me about Kirby. How did you find him?" Nelson motioned to a chair in the front room.

Tall wasn't sure how much he should tell. He, Levi, and Turon hadn't broke any laws. Even by crossing the line into Arkansas armed, they hadn't broken any. Tall's family culture and personal history prevented him from close association with law enforcement. Benton County had nothing on him, but he still was uneasy.

"A blue-eyed man came asking about a friend of

mine. Said he was buying cattle. My friend has a store on the upper end up by Spring Creek across the line. His name is Levi Kuratowski, folks call him Little Kansas."

"He's the man who caught Bill Kirby last year. I read about him in the paper. A fighter and store clerk." Nelson leaned forward interested.

"He's got a reputation for being a fighter." Tall smiled. "Only time he ever fought a man was the day he caught Kirby."

"If you are going to win a fight, that's the one to win," Nelson remarked.

"He was more interested in finding Levi than cattle. A few of us followed the blue-eyed man to a cabin between Spavinaw and Coon Creek this side of the line."

"It sounds like where that little nest of horse thieves operated. Cummings were their name. They cleared out last year in a hurry." Nelson made the chair creak as he adjusted himself.

"I rode in there and had an exchange with a redheaded woman who had been drinking. Overheard her talking to herself about Kirby. Got the impression Kirby had been staying there with the blue-eyed man and would be back soon.

"Kirby has reason not to like your friend. The people you are describing are Blue Tate and Molly O'Brien. Blue is a bootlegger and small-time criminal. I've heard he rode with various border trash in his past. Molly has had bad taste in men. She likes the rougher types. She's got a reputation up near Nebo but hasn't broken any laws we can prove. What makes you think Kirby is still in the area?" Nelson stood up and retrieved a tobacco pouch and papers from a shelf.

"There were fresh tracks leaving the place. Two sets. The corral had two mules. One, a pack mule from the looks of him. If he was leaving the country, I assume he would take the mules. I tricked the redhead into telling me this, Blue and another man rode off together." Tall declined the tobacco offered by the deputy Nelson.

"If she slipped up and told you anything, she must have been drinking." Nelson rolled a cigarette and wetted the edge of the paper. "I saw her on the witness stand once. She's sharp."

A knock at the door caught them both off guard.

"Who is it?" Nelson held the unlit cigarette waiting an answer.

"Howard. I have a reply from the marshal service."

Nelson left the lamp on the table and eased into the darkness near the door. Once again, he stood to the side of the door as it opened. Howard handed the note to Deputy Nelson.

"Might as well go home, Howard. Get some sleep." Nelson read the note before dismissing the telegraph operator.

"Yes, sir. Goodnight." Howard glanced at Tall and nodded.

Nelson handed Tall the note before disappearing through a dark doorway.

"Received. Do not engage. Marshal in route to Orchard City." Tall held the paper close to the lamp on the little table.

"Mr. Maul, since you sent the telegraph, I assume the 'do not engage' applies to you. Me, on the other hand, I do not intend to let riffraff like Blue and Molly consort with known criminals." Nelson walked back into the room with a boy of sixteen or so following close behind him.

"Listen here, James, go to Kelley's house and have him gather the association and meet me here by daylight. Then you ride to Bentonville." Nelson held a hand on the boy's shoulder. "Tell the sheriff Bill Kirby along with Blue Tate and Molly O'Brien are staying at the Cummings' old place on Coon Creek."

"Yes, sir." The boy nodded.

"Take Brownie. Once you have talked to the sheriff, hurry back here. Now get going." Nelson slapped the boy on the shoulder.

"The association?" Tall asked.

"Anti-Horse-Thief Association. It's a new civic organization in the area. They aid in the recovery of stolen animals. Pursuit of criminals across district lines."

Tall did not have a follow-up question. He had heard of the Anti-Horse-Thief Association. Knew what stood for justice for one class could mean injustice for another one. Not only did Tall avoid law enforcement, he avoided groups.

"I could have you deputized. You could ride with us."

"Wouldn't be legal. I'm a citizen of the Cherokee Nation." Tall reached down picking up his hat then continued. "I should be going. By the time I get home, I'll have stock to feed. I'm sure the wife is wondering where I am."

"If I need a sworn statement, how do I find you?" Nelson reached out a hand.

"Send word to Little Kansas' store. Someone there can find me." He shook hands with the deputy before excusing himself.

Tall climbed on his horse and rode out onto the dirt Main Street and turned him west.

Derrell the night watchman came into the street. "What did Nelson allow?"

"You are going to have several armed visitors by daylight." Tall reined up his horse, pausing by the watchman.

"I saw his boy ride off a minute ago."

"Go get a gun and horse and you may be able to

collect on the railroad reward."

"No, sir. More likely to get shot by one of those AHTA fellows. By the time they get here, I'll be in bed."

"Well, keep the risk low." Tall drummed his heels and the big horse stepped into a trot.

Chapter 16

Ruth's arms and legs were sore from riding tied up. She now faced the cabin the old men Glass and Wolf had described. From the cabin a yellow glow of light shown through the window and a loud voice of a woman singing could be heard.

"I hear something." Kirby reined up just before crossing Coon Creek.

"It's Molly. She must have found a jug," Blue said.

"You did say she gets careless when drinking, didn't you." Kirby urged his horse across the creek toward the sound of Molly's voice.

"In Dublin's fair city, Where the girls are so pretty, I first set my eyes on sweet Molly Malone, As she wheeled her wheelbarrow, through streets broad and narrow. Alive, alive, oh, alive, alive oh, crying cockles and mussels, alive, alive oh." Molly's voice carried into the darkness.

"Take care of the horses, Blue. I'll watch her." Kirby dismounted and took the rope Blue tied around Ruth's waist.

"I'll help you down, Miss Ruth." Blue climbed off his horse.

"No need, Blue." Kirby jerked the rope.

Ruth was unable to avoid the fall. With her hands tied behind her, she hit hard.

Her right shoulder absorbed the impact as well as her face as it crashed into the ground.

"Dang, Bill, why are you so rough?" Blue's voice was sharp rather than its usual genial tone.

"You may have forgotten, Blue, but she nearly took out my eye." Kirby squared off at Blue.

Blue took the horses into the corral. He was stashing the saddles in a lean-to shed when Kirby went to his, removed the carpetbag, and tucked it under an arm. The door of the cabin flew open. Molly held a lantern.

"Who are you?" Molly squinted into the darkness. "What you want?"

"We are back, Molly." Blue reached out to take her hand.

"Announce yourselves next time. I could have shot you." Molly's slap caught Blue across his face.

"How much have you had to drink?" Asked Blue as he rubbed his chin.

"Just enough to ease the pain in my ass you've caused me over the years."

Molly turned and went back into cabin.

Blue followed her inside. Kirby tugged on the rope, and Ruth, now on her feet, followed him with the obedience of a halter-broke colt. Kirby paused on the porch and pushed her inside before entering himself.

Molly started to speak but stopped upon seeing Ruth. She turned to Blue then Kirby.

"What happened to your eye?" Molly studied Kirby closely.

"This is Miss Ruth," Blue answered. "She took a swing at Bill."

"Shut up, Blue." Kirby shoved Ruth toward a bunk.

Molly looked Ruth over. Blood was dripping from the girl's nose and her attractive face smudged with dirt. Molly turned back at Blue then Kirby.

"You shitasses. You gone and kidnapped a Cherokee girl? Bad enough you got the federals after you. Now you want to get Indians after you?" Molly moved to Blue and swung a fist hard and fast.

Blue seeing it come, took a quick step back, and Molly followed her fist with the rest of her body. She crashed into the table sending kitchen implements flying. Including a knife that landed near Ruth.

Molly lay on her back. The table now missing a leg had given way under her weight. She slung utensils, pans, and plates away from her, attempting to stand up.

She fell once more and managed to stand up. She swayed a little and backed up to a bench. She sat down on one end of the bench, the other lifting off the ground. Sensing the bench out of balance, she quickly scooted over preventing toppling the bench and grabbing a jug she left there in one motion.

"You dumb shits." Molly took a long drink from the jug. "What are you going to do with her?"

"Never you mind." Kirby said as he walked past ignoring her.

Ruth was not sure what to do. She sat on the bunk while Kirby moved about gathering his belongings.

"Blue, your woman has eaten half my supplies." Kirby sorted through the food stores on a shelf.

"Our supplies, you shovel-jawed knothead." Molly took another drink from the jug.

"Oh, Molly, you're as tight as a fiddle string." Blue sounded defeated.

"I've only a had a few swigs to help against the night air." Molly scowled.

"All right, Molly." Blue lowered his head.

"What's the girl doing here?" Molly turned her scowl on Kirby.

"She's bait." Kirby finally spoke to her.

"What are you going to catch with her? A war party? Waw, waw, waw, waw, waw, waw." Molly raised her hand to her mouth and made slapping motions against her gaping mouth mimicking a war cry.

Kirby took a step toward Molly and raised a hand. Blue moved between them and the two men faced each other. Ruth watched with mild amusement. Her foot covered a knife that tumbled her way during Molly's drunken struggle to stand up. She slowly dragged it to the edge of the bunk.

"What are we going to do with the girl?" Blue added an edge of authority to his voice.

"I left a note. Told Little Kansas to come here, come here alone with a thousand dollars or we kill the girl." Kirby stood firm.

"See, Molly, he has a plan." Blue eased over to the bench and picked up the jug beside Molly.

Molly had an urge to pull Blue to her. His standing up to Kirby stirred something inside. Her jaw fell slack, and she began reddening around her neck and cheeks.

"So, we will take the money. Turn her loose and ride on?" Blue turned toward Kirby and took a drink.

"Something like that." Kirby glanced to Ruth and went outside carrying the carpetbag tucked under an arm.

"See, Molly? It's all planned out." Kirby sat the jug down on the bench out of easy arm's reach of Molly. "You better get some sleep if we are riding to Baxter."

"Why don't you come snuggle with me for a bit, Blue. It's frosty out." Molly reached out a hand and patted his thigh.

What Ruth thought would come next never did. Blue helped the redheaded Molly to a bed and in a minute, she was snoring. Blue checked the knots in Ruth's bindings. He pulled a blanket from a pack and draped it around her then went outside into the night.

Ruth sat still trying to hear the men outside. Molly snored the deep sleep snore of a drunk. Ruth eased herself to the floor and fingered the knife blade then handle, finally getting a hold on it. She rolled over and slowly stood up. Backing to the bunk, she sat back down on the bed.

She strained her ears to hear something, anything to warn her if either man came back in the cabin. Molly made a gasping sound. Ruth froze and Molly was soon snoring again. Deep, even snores.

Unable to use the knife with enough leverage to cut the rope, Ruth lay on her back. She flexed her hand and arms to the point she feared cutting circulation in her wrist. She could almost slip her hands below her waistline. Molly snored louder causing Ruth to stop and listen.

Hearing nothing except the sleeping Molly, she once again struggled. Straining, she began to feel pain like she'd never felt before. Her elbows, shoulders, and wrists all ached. Her muscles tensed throughout her lower body and trembled.

Finally, her tied hands slipped under and around her buttocks, and she tucked her knees into her chest bringing her hands in front of her. She sat breathing hard. Relieved to be in a better position. She held the knife, a well-worn butcher knife, in one hand running it under the rope. Her hands were numb, but she soon had the rope off.

She sat on the bed rubbing her hands together. Working the circulation back in. She tossed the cut rope aside then gathered them and stuffed them behind the bed. Leaving the rope around her waist in place, she tucked the knife behind her through the rope. The handle resting near the small of her back.

"What now?" she asked herself.

Molly continued to snore. Gas escaped her bowels when she rolled over once. Ruth sat in semidarkness plotting her next move. She stood up and eased toward the door. Movement at the window caught her eye. She could make out a shoulder. Blue or Kirby one was sitting on the porch. The cabin only had one door and one window. The man sat between both. She could hear the one called Blue speak.

"Bill. I'm ready to take down my shingle on this venture." Blue sat on the porch, his back to the wall.

"You're free to leave, Blue. Take your woman with you." Kirby stood with a rifle cradled in his arms watching the slope toward the creek.

"I'm ready to quit her too. I can't stay in this country now after kidnapping the girl with you. I don't want any more of this business." Blue flipped up his coat collar and crossed his arms across his chest against the chill of the night air.

"I'm not holding you here." Kirby leaned on a porch post and glanced at Blue.

"Will you turn the girl loose?" Blue asked.

"Sure. After I settle with the foreigner."

"What do you mean by settle? You took a risk coming here. Took a bigger risk bringing the Indian girl here."

"It's between him and me." Kirby still leaned on the porch post and watched the area now bathed in moonlight.

"If you are going to kill him, it's on you. The girl hasn't done anything to you. Why don't you let me take her away from here. She doesn't need to be a part of it."

"Molly might not like you sneaking off to the brush with an Indian girl." Kirby turned and glanced at Blue.

"I'm done, Bill. I just don't want anything to happen to the girl." Blue stood up, his knees popping as he did.

"Why do you care?"

"I'm tired of ugliness," Blue responded.

"What?"

"I used this place to run liquor but mostly to escape Molly. It's quiet here. Pretty the way the creek meanders below. Bringing you here then Molly and now the girl, I feel like I've ruined it. It was Molly's idea to take off and travel. I like it here. Now I can't stay."

Blue stepped off the porch and stared into the night.

"You can go right now if you want. If you stay, you stay until the end."

"Will you promise not to hurt the girl?" Blue watched the sky, his back to Kirby.

"I can't promise it. If she hits me again, I may stove her head in."

"If she doesn't try anything," Blue turned slowly to face him. "will you harm her?"

"I've got nothing against her. She's just bait at this point. I figure her falling from the horse made us even."

Kirby watched close, not sure what Blue would do.

"Well, Bill. I'm leaving. Let me gather a few things."

Blue marched toward the cabin door.

Ruth quickly moved back to the bunk. Her hands behind her as the cabin door opened. The man called Blue came in and picked up the lantern, shining the light on a bedroll and a canvas sack. He rummaged through the sack pulling a jar holding paper money and coins. He emptied the jar into a coat pocket. He hung the lantern in a metal hanger suspended from the ceiling.

Ruth could see Kirby standing at the edge of the doorway. Blue picked up a bedroll and stood before Ruth.

"You should get some sleep. You've had a hard evening. Bill has promised me he won't hurt you. Providing you don't get out of line. I'm sorry I roughed you and the boy up earlier."

Blue turned, paused briefly beside Molly, then disappeared through the open door.

Ruth watched as Kirby reached in and closed the door. She strained to hear any talk outside.

"You aren't going to go to the marshals or sheriff, are you?"

"You know me better than that, Bill." Blue picked up his saddle and tack.

Ruth pressed her face to the glass window and watched Blue catch and saddle the red mule. He took a length of rope and haltered his horse.

"If you are going to do what I think you will do, you all will have spare mounts. I'm taking Molly's mule and my horse." Blue led the animals through the gate then closed it.

"I always liked you, Blue, but you are too soft to ever make it in the world."

"Well, I can live with it. Take care of Molly. She will see you out of the country." Blue tied his bedroll behind the mule's saddle. Mounting the mule, he rode off to the north leading his tired horse.

Ruth watched from the window and could see Kirby standing with a rifle cradled in his arms. She considered her chances. The moonlight and cloudless sky provided enough light to make her a target if she ran. He would hear the cabin door open if she tried.

Kirby turned and eased onto the porch. She ducked below the window glass and hurried to the bunk. She heard him sit down against the wall. Her chance of escape now gone.

"Hogs going to get out." Molly spoke clear and sharp.

Ruth sat staring at the redheaded Molly as she rolled in her bed. A moment later, a soft consistent snore came from the drunk woman.

Ruth fingered the knife handle tucked in the rope behind her back. She could not see the stars and she had no watch but estimated it was a good hour before daylight. Milk time would be soon. She thought of Choogie.

"God, let Choogie be all right." Ruth talked low with her head bowed.

She didn't ask God for help for what she might have to do. She was not sure the creator would approve of what she had on her mind.

Chapter 17

Tall rode west on a prairie he had hauled freight across many times. Crossing the Arkansas state line and into the Cherokee Nation, he thought of the Sandusky farm ahead. The man Sandusky had a small farm and trading post.

"Another hour or so, he may have some coffee and a scoop of oats or corn for you, old Hoss." Tall patted the neck of his horse. "Coffee would hit the spot. But we better cut to the house." Tall held his pace and the big horse plodded on.

He skirted around the Sandusky place to avoid the yard dogs. Crossing a little hollow, he rode onto the Beck Prairie. He could make out the land's features in the moonlight. Movement caught his eye, and he could see horsemen. Three riders moving with purpose.

Tall slowed his horse. As they approached, it became clear their paths would collide. Something familiar about the riders made Tall want to announce himself but he waited.

A dun-colored mare one of the riders rode nickered giving away his location, and they reined up.

"Hello, *Syio*," Tall spoke in a friendly manner.

"Tall? Nearly took you for a tree." Turon urged his

dun mare forward.

"Where you all headed? What happened?" Tall recognized the other two riders as Ounce Pathkiller and John Turtle, Turon's father.

"Kirby. Him and the other fellow took Ruth and knocked Choogie in the head," Turon said.

"They what? Where's Little Kansas?"

"He took off after her. They left a note saying they had Ruth and to come to the cabin," Turon said.

"I thought you were watching the cabin." John Turtle moved his horse forward.

"I was. I heard the woman talking about Kirby. I slipped away and wired the marshals. A Benton County deputy is gathering members of the Anti-Horse-Theft Association. They are meeting at daylight in Orchard City." Tall felt as if he had messed up but could not decide how.

"How's Choogie?"

"He will be all right. Sore but alive." John pointed his rifle skyward as his horse pranced.

"We better get moving," Turon suggested.

The four riders rode in silence. A father with one child hurt and the well-being of another unknown. A son and brother propelled by loyalty to a friend and the protection of a sister. Two riders rode out of a kinship of community. Their own, not of blood but their own, were in danger. The four riders rode to uncertainty.

Levi stopped at a cast-iron post marking the boundary of the Cherokee Nation and the State of Arkansas. The mule's nostrils expanded and contracted sucking in air. The mare, although had made this trip twice already in the last twenty hours, appeared fresh. He swapped the saddle from the mule to the mare then let the animals rest for a few minutes more.

"Less than an hour until sunrise." He checked the stars to estimate how much time he had until daylight.

He pulled the revolver from his boot and checked the cylinders. Since carrying it, he habitually kept the chamber under the hammer empty. He now slipped a cartridge in place and shoved the revolver into his boot top.

He climbed into the saddle, the mare offering no opposition. Lifting the shotgun, he opened the action. He ran a thumb over the brass shell in the chamber then closed the action. He slipped the loop of rope over the saddle horn and suspended the shotgun there, barrel down. Urging the mare forward, he rode up the slope leading the mule. This was the last ridge before his path fell into the Coon Creek drainage.

He crossed a narrow clearing and rode around the head of a hollow before going down a timbered slope. Letting the mare pick her way down the hill toward the creek, he listened. Soon he was at the spot where he, Tall, and Turon had been the previous day. He dismounted and left the horse and mule tied to a downed tree. Staying in the shadows, he slipped closer to the clearing.

"Tall, I hope you are up there." Levi stared at the ridge above the cabin.

A light shown from the cabin window. The cabin itself stood out at the edge of the clearing. The pole corral held a few horses. One stood out. The black-and-white pinto gelding Ruth rode was there. He could make it out in the pale light.

Levi's heart pounded and he could hear the rush of its beating in his ears. Movement from the cabin caught his attention. A man was on the cabin porch.

"I wish I had a rifle," he said softly.

He studied the lay of the land. The cabin sat on a

slight rise. A clearing below the cabin led to the creek. Trees behind the cabin covered the ridge and really offered the only way of slipping in close unnoticed.

"Where's the second man?" Levi whispered.

If he did manage to get in the timber, he might mistake Tall for Kirby or the blue-eyed man. Or Tall might mistake him for one of them.

"They are expecting me. They will get me." Levi went to the little mare and climbed into the saddle, leaving the mule tied to the fallen tree.

Bill Kirby leaned against a porch post. He glanced at the cabin door and could hear Molly snoring. On a bench sat the carpetbag he had taken from the train a few weeks before. In it held enough money to last him years. Coughing from the cabin broke the snore cycle but in a moment, the snoring resumed.

He didn't check on the girl. He knew she would still be there. If she did escape the ropes, she could not escape the cabin without him seeing or hearing her. He turned his attention to the carpetbag. Sitting on the bench, he opened it and ran a hand through the currency.

"I don't need her to get me out of this country with all these frog skins." The night sky was surrendering to the predawn light as he continued. "Baxter Springs and a ticket out of here. I could make it by nightfall. If my horse held out." Kirby turned to the corral. "I could take the pinto too."

He stirred the money with a hand while staring off in the direction of Baxter Springs.

Revenge had plagued him for months. He could only think of how the little foreigner had managed to catch him off guard. His hand still stirred the money in the carpetbag.

"I reckon taking his woman is enough for now." Kirby closed the carpetbag snapping the clasp shut.

He went to the shed leaving the carpetbag on the bench. Grabbing his saddle, Kirby carried it to the corral. He wasted no time saddling his horse. He tied the pinto's lead rope to his saddle and led the animals to the cabin. He wrapped his horse's reins around a porch post with a half hitch, intending to go into the cabin and gather what few belongings he would need.

His mare turned her head and with ears forward, nickered. She made the reins tight straining the porch post. Kirby jerked his head up and heard the mare of the lone rider nicker in return before he saw Levi riding out to confront him.

"Isn't this just dandy." Kirby moved quick to the cabin door.

Ruth hurried to the bed and sat down with her hands behind her back. She grasped the knife handle still tucked in the rope she left around her waist. She had been watching through the little window and heard the mare nicker at an approaching rider.

The cabin door swung open, and the rifle barrel entered the room before the man. Kirby's eyes settled on Ruth and ignored the sleeping Molly.

"Behave yourself." Kirby held the rifle on Ruth and with his free hand reached and picked up the tail end of the rope still tied to her waist. "Try anything cute and you will answer for it."

He tugged on the rope, and she was on her feet. He thumbed the hammer back on the rifle. The audible click gave Ruth a chill down her lower back. Molly continued to snore.

"Let's move." Kirby stepped back outside the cabin, leading Ruth by the rope.

Ruth kept her hands behind her back and she did as

commanded. Her hand grasped the handle of the knife. Her breath caught short at the sight of Levi riding up the slope.

"That will be far enough." Kirby halted Levi forty yards away from him and Ruth.

"What did you do to her?"

"She felt sporty and took a swing at me. She's not so sporty now." Kirby held the rope in one hand but kept the rifle leveled at Ruth ten feet to his left.

"I'm fine, Levi." Ruth kept her back turned away from Kirby, concealing her hands and the knife.

"Shut up or I'll break your jawbone." Kirby tugged hard on the rope, jerking her a step toward him. "Did you bring the money?"

"If I said yes, would it matter?"

"You should have brought the money."

"I don't have it." Levi eased the mare forward a few yards.

"You little foreigners always have money. Gold and such." Kirby still held the rifle on Ruth.

"Why don't you let her go?" Levi continued to ease his mare a few yards closer.

"Stop right there." Kirby raised the rifle and steadied it on Ruth.

"Where's your partner? The blue-eyed man." Levi held his horse steady.

"He's about." Kirby eased the rifle back into the cradle of his arm.

"He took off hours ago." Ruth braced for the coming jerk of the rope.

"I said shut up." Kirby jerked the rope tight, but still remembering how she had leaped at him the night before kept her more than arm's length away.

Levi needed to be closer to have any chance with the shotgun or revolver. He moved his mare forward.

"You are trying to be tricky. Don't." Kirby still held

the rifle on Ruth.

"What do you want?" Levi yelled.

"A thousand dollars, if not, your hide. Add your little roan mare. I'm short on camp meat."

"Let her go and I'll stay. Just let her go." Levi held back his horse as she pranced.

"Levi, he'll kill you." Ruth did not brace herself when Kirby jerked the rope.

'That's it." Kirby narrowed his eyes then they widened with fear.

In close and under the rifle barrel, she brought the knife from behind her back. The swing and arch of the blade sliced through Kirby's coat and shirt. The tip of the knife running along a rib, flaying him to the bone.

In reaction to seeing her free hands then the knife, Kirby had tried to jump back. Involuntarily, he threw a hard punch his fist glancing off her shoulder as she swung around causing her to drop the knife. Her right arm now numb, she fell to the ground trying to grab the blade with her left hand.

"I'll going to kill you, you red hide—" Kirby did not finish his insult.

He heard the sound, and it froze him. A shout, more war cry, echoed in the morning air. The little foreigner called Little Kansas or who the Indian girl called Levi stood in the stirrups. His face contorted and the primeval roar coming from him. The little horse was in full gallop, her head and neck stretched out right at him. In her rider's hand, Kirby saw the revolver leveled at him and fire and smoke boomed from its barrel.

Abandoning all notions of attacking Ruth, he swung his rifle at Levi. His first shot wasted, he levered another round. Once more, the revolver spit fire and smoke. Kirby felt a stabbing-hot pain rip through his midsection then a thousand needle pricks of a rib bone shattering into his lungs.

Levi was unaware of the left swell of his saddle exploding and a burning sensation the bullet made tarring across his thigh. He leaned into the horse's momentum, and his right hand methodically chambered another round. Ruth was on her feet running for cover.

Kirby brought the rifle to his shoulder for his next shot. Smoke and fire roared from Levi's revolver as Kirby fired the rifle. His arm fell limp, the rifle falling to the ground. In anger, he commanded his arm to pick up the rifle only it lay out of reach. He bent down to reach it and felt tired. Sleepiness came over him, although his chest felt as if it was on fire. Stabs of pain tore at every breath. His legs crumbled under his weight. Sitting on the ground, he still commanded his arm to grab his rifle, but his arm betrayed him.

The bullet from Kirby's last shot hammered into the pistol grip, Levi's small finger taking the impact at full force. The lead round tumbled and tore down his arm holding the revolver. The right side of Levi's chest absorbing the bullet's impact. Trying to stop the mare, he slipped from the saddle. The ground came up hard as he fell like a rag doll. Dirt filled his mouth and he skidded to a stop.

The mare Kirby had tied to the porch post lunged against the rope. The post snapped and pulled loose sending the horse into a run dragging the post as it bounced beside her. The pinto's lead line snapped loose from the running horse, and he trotted back to the corral.

Through slitted eyelids, Kirby watched his horse run away. He could see the man called Little Kansas lying on the ground. Certain he had killed him, he tried to stand up, but his legs had no strength. On the porch under the now-sagging porch roof, he saw the red carpetbag. Making one more effort to stand, he instead lay down trying to catch his breath. A painful breath. Soon there was no pain. No breath.

Chapter 18

"Levi!" Ruth ran to his crumpled body. "Levi don't be dead."

She rolled him over carefully. Blood mixed with dirt as she tried to clean his face. Remembering a bucket of water in the cabin, she ran to it ducking under the sagging porch roof. The redheaded Molly still lay in her bunk oblivious to the morning events.

"Be alive." Ruth returned and washed the dirt from his mouth and face.

She held an ear to his chest. A slight rise and fall brought her joy, but fear soon replaced all hope. His left leg was bleeding. His right hand was now missing two joints of its pinkie. Flesh was torn along his right forearm, and blood was soaking his shirt below his armpit.

"Oh God, stay alive. Levi. I love you, Levi." Ruth held his head with one hand and slapped his face with the other.

"Ruth," Levi said barely audible.

"Levi?" She held her ear close to his mouth.

"Is Kirby dead?"

"He's dead." Ruth now gently caressed his face.

"Are you hurt?" Levi whispered.

"No, I'm fine, just fine," she said.

Levi's mare had not run away and came close to inspect her fallen rider before nickering and trotting to Ruth's pinto. The mare nickered again, and noise from the creek caught Ruth's attention. She laughed hard. Soon the tears came.

Turon's dun mare splashed through the creek, and the sun, now pouring over the high ridge, made the water sparkle. Ounce and her father flanked him, and the towering Tall on his black Percheron cross horse brought up the rear.

"Stay with me, Levi. Help is here." Ruth saw Levi's eyes close. "Levi! Stay awake, Levi."

Turon reached them first and jumped from the saddle.

"We're too late." Turon fell to his knees beside Levi.

"He's alive." Ruth's reaction was stern.

"Let me in there, back off." Tall lifted Turon from Levi's side.

Ruth backed away as the giant of a man ran his hands over Levi's thigh. Tall tore Levi's pant leg where the bullet had ripped a hole. He reached for the dipper in the bucket of water and splashed the wound.

"The redheaded woman had a jug yesterday. If there's whiskey in the cabin get me some." Tall shouted an order at Ruth and she ran to the cabin.

"Here." Ruth had sprinted to where Blue left the jug on the bench and returned.

"Leg's not bad. Ruth, tear me some cloth from your hemline or get me some flour sacks. As wide as your hand and long as your arm. Be quick, girl."

Tall tore Levi's shirt to examine his chest and arm.

"John, we need a travois. Get them boys busy. Use them poles from the corral. Ruth and I will plug up these holes."

Checking for busted ribs, Tall gently rolled Levi

over.

"Here."

Ruth had found the same knife she had cut the outlaw Bill Kirby with and was making strips for bandages.

Tall poured the whiskey on and into the bullet wound on the side of Levi's chest.

"The worst one is this hole in his side. I don't think it hit the lung, but we have to stop the bleeding." Tall took a strip of cloth from Ruth and jammed it into the bullet hole in Levi's side.

"He lost a finger too."

"He's not the only man hereabouts to lose a digit. There's enough of a stub to still count."

"Tall?" Levi mumbled.

"Thought you went under, kid." Tall wrapped longer pieces of cloth around Levi's chest and tied them tight.

Tall took a drink of the untaxed liquor and spit it to the side.

"It will do." He began pouring the whiskey on Levi's leg wound.

"Tall?" Levi winced and passed out.

"Will he make it, Tall?" Ruth sounded defeated.

"I've seen worse, girl. Much worse. Them boys will need a blanket for the travois and any rope you can find." Tall motioned toward the cabin and continued to clean the wounds with the whiskey.

Ruth jumped to her feet. She ducked under the sagging porch roof then entered the cabin. She went to the bunk where she had been and gathered two blankets. One being the same blanket Blue had placed around her. She scavenged the cabin for rope and found it. She paused only a moment. The odor of urine overwhelmed her nostrils and source of the smell dripped under Molly's bed to the floor. Ruth shook her head then left the sleeping redhead and rushed out the door. Her father tied two long poles together making a giant off-centered cross.

Turon found an axe and cut two shorter poles to serve as the bottom and top of the area where Levi would lay.

"Here you go." Ruth handed the blankets and rope to her father.

"Are you all right, are you hurt?" Her father took the blankets and rope in one arm and embraced her with the other one.

"I'm fine." Ruth still had dried blood on her face.

"Go see to your man," her father said.

Ruth hugged her father then rushed to Levi. Tall had Levi's leg bandaged and was holding a finger to Levi's throat.

"What are you doing to him?" Ruth was concerned and knelt beside Levi.

"Checking to see if his heart is still pumping. He's bled like a stuck hog."

Tall's eyes narrowed, and he studied Levi.

"Where did you learn to do this?" Ruth ran a finger over the neatly wrapped bandage.

"Stones River and later Shiloh." Tall stood and turned away. "Need the travois now, John."

Ounce led the black mule close by Levi. The travois tied to the pack saddle and the ends of the poles stuck out over the mule's head and the trailing ends dragging behind. A blanket stretched tight made a platform to lay Levi.

"We better wrap him in the other blanket. Tie him on so he doesn't move around." Tall waved a hand at the second blanket.

Ruth grabbed the blanket and spread it out beside Levi. Tall lifted Levi and sat him on the blanket. As swaddling a baby, he wrapped him. Not waiting on help, Tall gathered Levi in his arms and laid him on the travois.

Turon took some rope and tied Levi to the travois so he would not slip during transit.

"He needs a pillow or something to keep his head still." Ruth inspected the rope.

Ounce commented in Cherokee and sprinted to the cabin. Returning, he handed Ruth a red carpetbag.

"That should work." Turon lifted Levi's head.

Ruth tucked the red carpetbag behind and around Levi's neck. Whatever was in the bag was easy to form and secured his head.

John Turtle stood over the body of Bill Kirby. He reached down and picked up the rifle. Opening the action, he looked down the barrel and checked for dirt and debris. Seeing none, he closed the lever. A revolver was stuck in Kirby's waistband, and he pulled it out and stuck it in his own.

Turon picked up Levi's revolver from the ground then mounted his horse. He rode up taking the lead line of the little black mule. Ounce led the saddled pinto to Ruth for her to ride.

"The closest doctor is in Row." Tall mounted his big horse.

"Let's go." Turon urged his dun mare forward leading the little black mule of Kirby's.

Ruth rode behind the mule so she could keep an eye on Levi. Tall rode beside her leading Levi's mare. John Turtle retrieved Choogie's mule from where Levi had left him tied.

Ounce studied the place and took time to wipe out the tracks the travois made to the creek. He found Kirby's sorrel mare and untied the porch post it was still dragging. He removed the hackamore and saddle. The hackamore he hung on his saddle horn, and he tucked Kirby's saddle under his arm. Kirby's mare was grazing when he rode away. Leaving no sign any of them had been there.

Molly awoke. Her mouth felt cracked and dry. She coughed and worked her tongue trying to lubricate her mouth to form words.

"Blue?" She sat on the edge of the bed with her head in her hands.

"Blue?" Coughing, she stood up.

"What the hell happened?" She vaguely remembered the table breaking.

Not finding the jug on the bench, she reached for the coffeepot sitting on a cold stove. Pulling the lid from the pot, she tilted the pot and drank long and hard. Sitting the pot down and dropping the lid, she felt her stomach churn and her throat muscles loosening. She realized in a moment she needed to vomit. Out of muscle memory and old habit, she ran for the open door to throw up outside. The roof of the porch now hung low only five feet above the porch boards. The five-foot-four-inch Molly in a sprint caught the oak porch header with the full force her weight generated.

Hungover, soiled, and with a self-inflicted head wound, she passed out and fell hard to the porch boards. Her body rejecting the cold coffee and grinds along with what contents had remained in her stomach now drenched her. Unaware her Blue had abandoned her. Unaware her meal ticket Bill Kirby lay dead twenty yards from her. Unaware the fortune she coveted was now a pillow for a gravely wounded man.

Chapter 19

"Hunting accident my ass."

The doctor studied Tall for a reaction.

"How he got shot doesn't really matter, does it?"

"No. Does he have papers out on him? Warrant?"

The doctor carefully cleaned the wound on Levi's side.

Tall gave the doctor a disappointing look.

"I know," the doctor continued. "It doesn't matter."

"He's not wanted," Tall reassured the doctor. "Just had an accident."

"Does his shooting have anything to do with this girl?" The doctor motioned toward Ruth. "Wouldn't be the first shotgun proposal gone wrong," he continued.

"Is he going to live?" Ruth asked, ignoring the doctor's question.

"He's lost a lot of blood. You all did a respectable job stopping the bleeding. I am afraid his finger will not grow back. Hope he wasn't a banjo player."

The doctor picked up a needle and thread.

"Will he live?" Ruth was irritated.

"He survived the Indian drag carriage here. He may survive my stitch job. He's a tough lad. Infection will be the only worry now. He will need to stay here for a week. I'd say if we can keep the wounds from getting infected, he will be fine. Using the whiskey to clean the injuries was smart. It will help stave off infection." The doctor focused on his work stitching Levi's side.

Ruth bit her lip watching the doctor jab the needle in and out of Levi's skin.

"Now you two go downstairs and let me work. I'll come get you if he wakes up. Right now, his body needs rest, and I need to finish my sewing while he's still out. Go on now."

They lingered near the door for a while before stepping out on the stair landing. Ruth followed Tall down a steep narrow set of stairs on the outside of the building.

"Never understood why doctors put their offices on the second floor. Sure hard to get folks in trouble upstairs." Tall kept his footsteps on the side of the steps above the bracing, the boards creaking under his weight.

"How is he?" Turon asked from where he had been waiting under the stairs.

"Doc says we got him here in time. He wants to hang on to him for a week."

Turon had disassembled the travois and laid the poles beside the building. The carpetbag rolled up in the blankets was tied behind Ruth's saddle on the pinto.

"Pa went home to check on Choogie and tell Momma you're safe." Turon paused, watching his sister. "You should get home yourself."

"Someone should stay here." Ruth looked up to a second-floor window. "In case he wakes up."

"He's in good hands. Doc can be coarse to converse with but he's a good doctor," Tall reassured her.

"I can now die knowing I met the approval of Tall Maul." The doctor closed the door and stood on the stair landing.

The three looked up at the doctor. He struck a match on the stair railing and lit a pipe. Smoke building as he puffed.

"All of you appear as though you need rest. He will be in fine care. I'll send a boy to Tall's place if he makes a turn for the worse."

"When can I see him?" Ruth asked.

"Come back this time tomorrow. Bring the lad some fresh clothes." The doctor opened the door and went back inside.

The three rode out of Row across the prairie. Riding in silence for there was nothing to say. Turon led Levi's mare and the little black mule belonging to the dead Kirby followed, although Turon had turned him loose.

"Should we go to the sheriff?" Ruth finally broke the silence.

"What happened, happened in Arkansas. If they have questions, they can come to us." Tall said. "As for the sheriff. He doesn't care what happens in Arkansas."

"The woman in the cabin passed out. She seen me last night."

"I doubt she wants to admit to kidnapping. Deputy Nelson can sort it out. I bet them Anti Horse Theft Association boys are already splitting up the reward money for Kirby. If they have questions, they know where to find me."

"It's over, then. Kirby's dead," Ruth spoke as if checking off an item on a chore list.

"Just need Levi to rally," Turon said.

"He will. He must." Ruth turned in the saddle and moved the rolled blankets back to the center and made the saddle strings tighter.

"Why did you keep these blankets and carpetbag?"

"Seemed like good blankets, just need a wash. Carpetbag is a good bag. Might be useful one day.

Seemed a shame to leave them."

"Waste not. Want not," Tall said, eying Ruth. "Good to see thrift in the younger generation."

They rode west down into a little valley then crossed Clouds Creek. Climbing a steep ridge up a cow trail they were out on another prairie dotted with giant post oaks.

"Turtle cattle." Tall motioned to a little black cow with upright horns and carrying the Turtle brand on her hip.

"The calf needs a matching brand. This building a store and chasing outlaws has gotten in the way of my cattle empire." Turon watched the big bull calf with white foam dripping from its mouth.

"I can get Toe and Lee to help. We can start whenever you are ready. I've got a few head I need to locate myself," Tall said.

"I will get with Ounce and the neighbors. We need to start before fly season. It will be here soon." Turon scanned the horizon for more cattle carrying the Turtle brand.

Tall left Turon and Ruth and rode west to his home place as the siblings rode south across the Long Prairie toward Spring Creek. They had to pass the store on their way. There, the old men Glass and Wolf sat under their oak watching the younger Toe and Lee work. Toe setting stones in place and Lee lowering the stones down with a rope.

"Turon, Ruth." Lorelei ran from the store building.

Turon jumped from the saddle and caught her in his arms.

"I am so happy to see you." Lorelei's eyes glistened. "How's Levi?"

"Doctor thinks he will be fine. Just needs rest. How is Choogie?" Turon held her tight.

"Choogie is fine. He has a headache. He was trying to steal a horse when I left the place this morning. Said he was going to ride out to find you. Your momma nearly had to sit on him to keep him home."

"I'm happy he's going to be all right. You opened the store?" Ruth watched a family she knew carrying some supplies to a buckboard wagon.

"Your momma wanted to keep me busy, I think. She sent me here. Said we must keep grinding."

"I can help you." Ruth slid down from the saddle.

"You should go home and rest. I'm managing fine," Lorelei protested.

"I need something to do myself. Turon can let Momma know I'm here and safe."

"I'll take him home, Ruth. See he gets some grain and rubbed down. I'll be back later today to bring you two home." Turon took the pinto's reins from Ruth.

"I'll draw some water and heat you some so you can freshen up." Lorelei realized, as did Turon, there was no use to argue with Ruth.

Turon spoke briefly to Toe and Lee. The old men Glass and Wolf came over, and Turon nodded to the black mule still following behind. Glass caught the mule and inspected its teeth.

Turon rode on leading the pinto and Levi's little roan mare. The black mule stayed with its new owner. As Old Man Glass patted his head.

When the water in the pot was warm to the point of discomfort, she carried it to the back room of the store where Levi had built his living quarters. Ruth had searched his meager belongings and laid out a set of clothes she could take to the doctor's office in Row the next day.

"There is stew left over and bread. I'm sorry, I should have thought of it already." Lorelei sat the pot of warm water along with a rag next to a wash basin on a small counter built into a wall.

"Thank you, I could eat."

"I'll be right back." Lorelei went to the front of the store.

Ruth washed her face. The warmth of the soaked rag felt good. She opened her blouse and wiped from her neck down.

Lorelei returned carrying a bowl of stew and sliced bread. She returned to the storefront upon hearing a customer. A few minutes later, she returned with a cup of coffee for Ruth.

The two young women sat together. Ruth told the events of what happened. Lorelei did not quiz her. Just let Ruth talk at her own pace while she ate. Lorelei could see she was exhausted. Retelling the events of the previous night seemed to exhaust her more. Lorelei took the bowl and cup from Ruth.

"Lay down for a bit. If I need help, I will get you." Lorelei placed the dishes aside and offered a hand to Ruth.

"He was so weak." Ruth took her hand and stood up trembling a little.

"He is strong. He's got a strength in him unmatched. I've seen it before. He will be all right. We will pray for him to be all right." Lorelei was ready and caught Ruth in her arms as they embraced.

They stood for a minute. The two would have been strangers a year earlier; now sisters, they held each other. Ruth admitted she could lie down, and she staggered to the narrow bed Levi had built himself. His bedroll blankets from his cowboying days stretched tight across the bunk.

Ruth sat on the edge of the bed and ran her hand over the wool weave. She extended her hand and ran it under the goose down pillow as she lay down. From under the pillow, she pulled out Levi's tallit and clutched it. She laid down her head. She could smell his scent on the pillow where his head had laid. She closed her eyes and held tight to his prayer cloth. Sleep overcame her before Lorelei could close the curtain separating the living quarters from the store.

"I heard Pa say Kirby was dead." Choogie stood on a crate brushing Levi's mare.

"He's dead." Turon brushed the taller pinto.

"Little Kansas killed him in a gunfight?" Choogie pressed Turon for the details.

"He did. If anyone asks, you don't know anything about it."

"I wish I had been there to see it." Choogie plucked a burr from the mare's tail.

"Good way to get shot," Turon said. "Watching gunfights."

"I wish I could have seen it. I miss everything." Choogie went back to brushing the mare's coat.

"Here, take these horses to the corral. See they get some corn. You won't have to miss that." Turon handed him the lead lines for the pinto and little dun mare.

Mumbling, Choogie led the horses through the barn to the corral. Turon thought of the blankets he had stowed behind Ruth's saddle. He pulled the loose ends of the saddle strings and untied the blankets and carpetbag. Pulling the carpetbag from the bundle, he opened it curious as to what was inside.

A minute passed. Turon stared into the carpetbag.

"The train money."

He wandered over to a bench and picked up a flour sack Choogie had been using for some reason unknown to Turon. He emptied the money into the sack. He stood thinking of what to do. Remembering an empty grease tin, he lifted the lid off. The sack bulged over the rim of the tin. He pushed down, packing the cash in place and snapped the lid down shut.

He strolled to the little cabin he shared with Lorelei. As he passed his parents' house, he dropped the blankets and empty carpetbag on the porch.

Inside the little cabin in the rafters, a little platform held items, totems from Turon's boyhood. Beside the wood chest holding these treasures, Turon placed the tin of money. He lay down with an arm behind his head. Stretched out, he studied the tin's resting place.

Chapter 20

Molly rode in the wagon, her legs crossed and arms folded. The body of Bill Kirby lay wrapped in a blanket in the wagon bed. The body tilted and rolled against her knees with the uneven ground.

"Not fitting for a woman to ride with a dead man." The farmer grumbled and flipped a rein over the back of the left wheeler horse of the team.

"Not fitting for a woman to smell like that. You want her to ride next to you?" Deputy Nelson rode beside the wagon.

"Reckon not." The farmer glanced back at Molly.

Behind the wagon, members of the Anti-Horse-Thief Association rode in silence. Molly glared at them. Her head ached and a knot bulged at her hairline.

"Brave lot, you are. Capturing a poor woman." Molly kicked the body of Bill Kirby away as it rolled against her. "What are you going to do with me? Captain Nelson?" she said with contempt.

"Just Deputy Nelson, Mrs. O'Brien."

"Well, Deputy. What are you going to do with me?" Molly used the same level of contempt at the word deputy.

"Just taking you to the sheriff. He'll ask you some

questions."

"What questions?" Molly sounded irritated.

"How you ended up in the company of a dead outlaw for one. Another is how did he die?" Deputy Nelson eyed Molly for a reaction.

"Consumption more than likely," Molly said.

"Consumption?" Deputy Nelson turned and studied the redheaded Molly. "How's that?"

"Appears he consumed one too many bullets." Molly glare at the deputy.

A few of the riders behind the wagon laughed.

"You have a smart mouth, Molly." The deputy drummed his heels and set his horse into a trot to be away from her sight and smell.

"We may need to ride upwind," one of the riders said.

"Go to your eyeballs, you logger-headed bastard." Molly shot the man a sharp glance.

Late in the afternoon, the wagon and escorts entered the square in Bentonville, Arkansas. Once called Osage, it was the seat of government of Benton County. Tucked in the corner of the courthouse, the sheriff's office had a side entrance. The farmer halted his team even with the door.

"Nelson, who did you capture?" A middle-aged man in a dark suit approached the wagon.

"A client maybe." Nelson dismounted and slipped a lead line through an iron ring of a hitch post.

"Madam, I advise not incriminating yourself and secure council." The attorney in the dark suit tilted his hat at Molly.

"I'm fresh out of hogs." Molly dismissed the attorney.

"Is that evidence wrapped in the blanket?" The attorney motioned to the body in the wagon.

"It's Bill Kirby." Deputy Nelson strode to the tailgate

of the wagon.

"You don't say." The attorney moved closer.

"Climb on out, Molly, we will visit the sheriff." Deputy Nelson dropped the tailgate open.

Molly stood in the wagon bed and moved Kirby's body out of her way with her foot and slowly moved to the wagon's tailgate. There she squatted and jumped out landing on her feet. None of the men offered to help her. The attorney stuck his snout of a nose into the air and retreated a few yards.

"Good luck, Deputy. Ma'am." The attorney tilted his hat once more and strolled down the sidewalk.

"Let's go, Molly." Deputy Nelson motioned her toward the door of the sheriff's office.

"Yes, sir. Deputy."

"If you could do me another favor. Take the body over to Basinger's Funeral Home," Deputy Nelson said to the farmer.

"Sure, sure thing." The farmer spoke to his team, and the wagon moved down the street.

The members of the Anti-Horse-Thief Association tied their horses and filed to some benches awaiting any statements they may have to make. Deputy Nelson escorted Molly through the sheriff office's door.

"Nelson, come on in." The sheriff eased back in his chair expression cheerful.

Upon seeing Molly, his expression changed, and he stood up with a more serious expression on his face.

"Mrs. O'Brien, what brings you to town?" The sheriff greeted her and offered her a seat.

"A wagon and this son of a bitch's gun." Molly sat in the chair and jerked a thumb toward the deputy.

"I'll have none of that kind of talk. Did you hit her?" the sheriff questioned Nelson.

"We found her in this condition," Deputy Nelson said.

"Why is she here?" The sheriff sat in his chair.

"A citizen in the Cherokee Nation came to me last night. He said he had reason to believe Bill Kirby was staying in a cabin on Coon Creek with Blue Tate and Mrs. O'Brien here." Nelson motioned at Molly.

"Your boy got word to me. I had to be in court this morning. I assumed you could handle it."

"Wasn't much to handle. We split our party and moved in from the ridge above the cabin and the creek below. We found Bill Kirby dead. Shot twice and cut open with a knife." Nelson pointed at his own chest in two places and made a slicing motion with a thumb at his ribs.

"Dead?" The sheriff let out a low whistle.

"There were signs of a struggle. Blood on the ground and Bill Kirby lying dead still warm. Found her passed out on the porch. Her head banged up. The roof of the porch had fallen, a porch post missing."

"Care to add anything Mrs. O'Brien?" the sheriff asked.

"I don't know anything about a Bill Kirby. I thought his name was Hawkins. Blue was finding cattle for him to buy in the Nations."

"What happened to your head?" the sheriff asked.

"I was in the cabin asleep. I heard a noise and ran outside. The porch roof must have fallen, and I ran into it. I don't remember anything else." Molly crossed her arms.

"Johnson." The sheriff yelled for a deputy to come in the office, and he appeared in a sprint. "Escort Mrs. O'Brien down the hall to the washroom. Have her wait outside when she's finished. Do you need a doctor, Mrs. O'Brien?" the sheriff asked politely.

"No." Molly stood up and stomped out of the room with Deputy Johnson by her side.

"Close the door, Nelson." The sheriff motioned with

his chin to the door.

"Before I question her any more, I want to hear what you think." The sheriff leaned back in his chair.

"I think Kirby, Blue, and this woman were conspiring to rob another train or a bank. Something happened. An argument or fight over something. Kirby has a swollen black eye. Someone hit him a good one. If you got a good nose full, it's plain she had been drinking. The two men fought early in the morning. Knocked the porch roof loose or a horse pulled it loose based on the tracks. She ran out to see what was wrong and hit her head on the porch beam. Soiled and vomited all over herself then passed out."

"Kirby was supposed to have money." The sheriff eased forward in his chair and scratched the back of his head.

"We tore the place apart. Except for Molly, six jugs of whiskey, and a sorrel mare, there was nothing else."

"What about the guy who told you Kirby was in the area?" The sheriff pulled a ruler from his desk and scratched between his shoulder blades.

"Tall Maul, he's a freighter and has an Indian wife in the Nations. He's not mixed up with the likes of Blue Tate or Molly."

"It appears to me, Blue finally got the nerve to run off from Molly. When he did, I think him and Kirby must have fought and Blue won. I would be willing to wager Blue is over in the Nations now with the money from the train robbery."

"Do you think she could have killed Kirby?" The sheriff returned the ruler to his desk.

"She is capable of killing us all. But she didn't kill Kirby. There wasn't a gun on the place. Only a butcher knife lying on the ground. I assume it was used to cut Kirby's side open. Even if she used the knife, it wasn't enough to kill him. Two bullet wounds did." Nelson hooked his thumbs in his belt and leaned against the wall.

"Get her statement on paper and have her sign it. If she signs it, she can go home for now."

"Let her go?" Nelson stood up off the wall.

"Other than the whiskey, there's not much to charge her with."

"She might know where Blue has gone," Nelson said.

"If she does, she won't tell us. If she takes off, then we will follow her. Johnson was complaining about his wife earlier. Maybe five or six days of camping in the brush will cure him. If she does takes off, then she will lead us to Blue. If she doesn't know where he is, then good for Blue." The sheriff stood and went to a window.

"Some of the association boys are outside. They are willing to write statements on what we discovered."

"Good deal. Get their statements. Get hers and turn her loose. I'll visit with Johnson and tell him the good news." The sheriff moved to the stove, toed open the stove door, and tossed a stick of wood on the fire.

"I am sure he will be thrilled." Nelson retrieved a moleskin notebook.

Molly refused the offer of Deputy Nelson to let her sleep the night in a cell and a ride home the next morning. It was late in the afternoon when she started plodding to her farm west of Nebo on Beaty Creek. Eighteen miles she had to cover before she would be home.

"Blue, I'll kill you if I ever find you." She marched down the road ignoring glances from people passing by.

"Bet he got sweet on the Indian girl. Either turned her loose or ran off with her." Her head pounded and her mood worsened.

"Kirby must have caught him. Why didn't he wake me, then? Why did he take the money and not take me?"

Molly picked up a rock and threw hard, hitting a yard dog in the ribs who came out to the road to bark at her.

"He didn't take me. After all I have done for him. He didn't take me with him." Tears trickled down her face. "He even took my mule."

Down the road she trekked. Her money was all gone. Kirby's money was gone. Blue was gone and Kirby dead. Her head pounded and stomach ached. After a mile, she had no more tears. Her feet grew sore. Mile after mile, she hiked as the afternoon stretched into evening.

"Shitasses." She cursed Benton County. She cursed all men to hell. "Shitasses, all of them. Shitasses."

Chapter 21

"Just because you are a store clerk now doesn't mean you should dodge real work." Turon said holding the door open.

"You would think you could manage without me for a week." Levi emerged from the doctor's office onto the stair landing.

The air was cool, but the sun felt warm against the white two-story building. He had begun to go stir crazy by day two. Ruth and Turon both had come to see him. Ruth brought food everyday once he had kept some of the doctor's thin soup down. The doctor had been strict about keeping the wounds clean. Confined to the upstairs, Levi had witnessed the doctor's practice.

Day three, he got to see the doctor set a broken arm of a ten-year-old boy. The cracking sound of the bone going back into place and the cry of the boy as he bit down on a leather strap stuck with Levi.

It was later in the day the doctor discovered Levi knew how to play chess. This brought on a new dynamic as the doctor was starved for a chess match. Levi hadn't played in years but soon remembered openings he had long forgotten.

Day six, Levi had worried the doctor was keeping him prisoner to only play chess. When Ruth had brought a basket of food early in the afternoon, Levi thought it was the daily food delivery keeping him hospital bound. As Ruth prepared to leave, the doctor told her he saw no reason Levi could not go home the following day.

Levi's thigh was sore, but he managed the stairs fine. The wound on his sided itched awful, but he had grown to ignore it under the doctor's constant orders not to scratch it. The most painful and frustrating wound was his bandaged little finger. With the new set of clothes Ruth insisted he put on before they left, he didn't appear banged up too bad.

"If you get fevered, get back here on the quick or fetch me." The doctor said standing on the stair landing. "I'll be by your way in a week or so to check you out. I'll bring a chess board."

"Thank you, Doctor," Levi said before climbing into the wagon.

"No, thank you." The doctor folded the money Turon gave him and tucked it into a vest pocket before he disappeared back inside his office.

"I'll pay you back when we get to the store." Levi took a seat.

"I nearly forgot." Ruth grabbed a basket of cookies from under the wagon seat and ran up the stairs to the doctor's office.

"I should have been a doctor," Levi said as she returned to sit beside him.

"Still can if you want." Ruth unwrapped the reins from the brake handle.

"Not if I have to set bones."

"You missed the roundup." Turon swung into the saddle of his bay horse.

"I know. I feel bad about it," Levi said.

"Well, we branded your calves." Turon urged his bay forward. "All three head. All heifers."

"Calves?" Levi grabbed the wagon seat with his good hand as Ruth flipped the reins across the backs of the team, starting them moving.

"Yup, branded your forty-below brand on them. Marked their ears with a swallow fork on the right side." Turon eased his bay back and rode even with the wagon.

"I don't have any cattle." Levi sat with his feet braced on the foot board trying to avoid any jarring movements.

"You do now. Gee a little bit, Sam." Ruth flipped the reins again and talked to the team.

"Ruth has three cows she raised from calves. She claims what's yours is hers and what's hers is now yours." Turon grinned.

"I see." Levi studied the horizon.

"You backing out now?" Ruth questioned Levi.

"No. It's the only way I get to keep my pup, Moses."

"Mo," Ruth corrected him.

They left Row and traveled south around the Clouds Creek drainage avoiding the deep hollow to the west. Away from townspeople and out on the prairie, Levi finally asked, "What about Bill Kirby?"

"Tall talked to the deputy the other day. He came out to where we had some cattle gathered."

"What did he say?" Levi asked.

"They seem to think Blue Tate. The blue-eyed man must have gotten into a fight with Kirby and ridden off after shooting him dead."

"What if they find Blue Tate?" Levi asked.

"Does not concern us. It's Arkansas' business and the federals."

"What about me being in the doctor's office?"

"Terrible accident. We all worried about you. You should have known better and checked the shotgun before shooting at the turkey," Turon scolded.

"Turkey?"

"Yeah, big tom turkey down on the creek. We figure a dirt dabber must have built a nest in the barrel last year. Went to make a hurried shot and the breech exploded. Lost part of a finger, and shrapnel lodged in your chest. Good thing we found you in time."

"Just like that?" Levi asked.

"Just like that, Levi." Ruth gave him a sharp glance then smiled.

"Pa, Ounce, Tall, and I will swear on the Bible it's what happened." Turon continued to ride beside the wagon.

"You shouldn't have to lie." Levi's expression was somber.

"We aren't lying if nobody asks. The territory is a better place without Kirby in it."

"I should have checked the shotgun before taking off after the turkey," Levi said.

"Yeah, bet you don't do it again." Turon laughed.

"No. Bet I don't." Levi absentmindedly scratched his wound then dropped his hand from it.

"I'm going to ride ahead. You two don't be long." Turon drummed his heels urging his bay into a short lope.

"Wonder why he's in a hurry?" Levi watched Turon ride away.

"Lorelei is watching the store. He's just going to check on her." Ruth flipped the reins over the team's backs.

"How is the store?"

"Great. Busier than ever. We are running low on some supplies; we need to put in an order soon. The spring weaves are selling fast. Folks are sewing spring and summer dresses already."

"I'm not sure what I would have done without you, Ruth."

"No telling. I moved your little narrow bed out and put a bigger bed in the back room. Toe and Lee built a wardrobe; it will do for now. Also got rid of the curtain you were using for a door." She slapped the leather lines across horses rumps. "Haw a little, Tom, straighten up." Ruth talked to the team.

"What was wrong with my bed?"

"It was too little for both of us. For sleeping anyway." Ruth smiled.

"Figured you would sleep at your folks' place for the time being. I only own two sets of clothes. Don't see why I need a wardrobe."

"Are you sure you aren't backing out of marriage?"

"I thought you wanted a June wedding?"

"Sooner may be better." Ruth shrugged.

"Glad to see I no longer have to make any decisions." Levi started to scratch his wound then stopped.

"Turon said you were smart for a white boy." Ruth broke into laughter.

Levi frustrated now sat in silence. Ruth teased him, and he finally caved and cracked a smile. He saw the tall oak first then followed by the roofline of the store. The closer they got, Levi could make out horses and wagons.

"Lorelei must be doing a lot of business."

As they neared the store, he counted a dozen wagons and three times as many horses. Men were playing baseball while women and children watched. Smoke from cook fires drifted across the playing field.

"What's going on?" Levi asked.

"People are glad to see you alive." She drove the team in close to the store.

Levi eased himself down from the wagon and was on the ground before Ruth could offer to help him.

"*Siyo*, I'll take care of the team and wagon." Ruth's father welcomed Levi back and led the team around to the side of the store.

The baseball game continued, even though some of the crowd came over to greet them. Many spoke in Cherokee, and Levi only understood a word here and there. Ruth, who normally translated for him, had disappeared.

Turon trotted over from the baseball field. "Little Kansas, got someone I need to introduce you to." He ushered him toward the giant oak tree.

"What's the score?" Levi asked, as a wood slat cracked against a ball.

"Zero to nothing the last I checked." Turon motioned to a barrel-chested Cherokee in a dark suit of clothes.

"Little Kansas, this is the Reverend Cochran. He's an old friend of the family and has the little church out west of here."

"Little Kansas." The Reverend reached out to Levi, and they shook hands.

"Levi Kuratowski. Folks call me Little Kansas."

"It is nice to meet you at last. I've heard a lot about you. You will need to visit us on Sunday." Reverend Cochran waved a hand summoning a Cherokee man to come over. "You're in luck. Normally, you would need to go to the courthouse to get a license, but Dennis is court clerk for the Goingsnake district. Ruth explained your situation. Glad to see you on your feet."

"License?" Levi was confused.

"Dennis, here's the young man." Reverend Cochran motioned to Levi.

"Dennis Blackfox, heard a lot about you. Glad you are settling here. I just need you to sign here. Turon, will you stand as witness?"

"Sure." Turon took the paper and laid it on a wagon tailgate nearby.

"Here you go." The court clerk produced a fountain pen.

"Here, Little Kansas." Turon offered Levi the pen after signing his name.

"I thought I already had a business license." Levi talked low as he took the pen from Turon.

"You do. Read the header. What do you think this all is about?" Turon spoke so only Levi could hear him.

"Certificate of Marriage Goingsnake District of the Cherokee Nation." Levi turned the paper and read the header.

"Well, what a sight." The court clerk Blackfox let out a low whistle.

Levi turned to see what caught the court clerk's attention. In a white gown, Ruth came down the steps of the store's porch. The crowd parted as she sashayed toward the giant oak tree. Levi stood dumbfounded with pen in hand.

"You going to fish or cut bait?" Turon grinned at Levi.

Levi leaned over the tailgate and signed the marriage certificate.

"Congratulations, Mr. Kura, Kura, Little Kansas, congratulations." The court clerk shook Levi's hand.

Ruth moved with grace directly to Levi. They stood staring at each other under the giant oak. Turon grabbed the edge of a wagon board and jumped into the bed. He cupped his hands and let out a yell.

"Once these two are married we can eat," he shouted and jumped to the ground.

People gathered around the couple under the giant oak. Reverend Cochran stood in front of Ruth and Levi. His stern gaze hushed the crowd.

“This is your last chance to run.” Ruth reached and took Levi’s hand.

“I told you. It is the only way I can keep Moses.”

“Mo,” she corrected him.

Afterword

As in the first book of this series the characters are fictional. Certain family names may sound familiar if you live or are from the area where this story takes place. The geography is correct, and all the places existed at that time. Many still exist. Although much of it is on private property. There are places you can check out, and I encourage you to do so.

Prisoners of Judge Parker's court in Fort Smith would have been transported by train to Detroit, Michigan and a federal penitentiary like the Kirby character. Although the majority would serve their time, there are examples of prisoners escaping trains. Pretty Boy Floyd famously dove through a window as a train crossed a creek leaving federal agents stunned and unable to pursue.

Today the Arkansas Missouri Railroad offers excursions on the same rail line that carried Belle Starr to prison. Although you cannot make connections to Detroit, you can ride from Springdale to Van Buren, Arkansas through the scenic Boston Mountains. Book your tickets early if you plan to take your ride during the autumn. In historic downtown Van Buren you will find restaurants and plenty of shopping before you ride the train back to Springdale.

In 1999 the cast iron post still stood on the state line just south of Coon Creek west of Arkansas highway 43. It was on private property then and I have no idea if it still stands today. I hope it does. If I remember correctly the date stamp on the post was 1876. There would have been several along the border of Arkansas and Indian Territory.

The ridge between Coon and Spavinaw Creek is a private residence now. When I was kid, I frequented a swimming hole just below where the fictional Cummings cabin stood above Spavinaw Creek. I learned to swim there as did many people. Once when I was fourteen, I walked around a bend and came across a young Cherokee woman bathing. I remember her copper toned skin and jet-black hair. It was a brief encounter for she moved into deeper water, her modesty restored. Out of respect I retreated downstream along with the soap foam.

Spavinaw was cold, and in a world before air conditioning was common it provided relief in the summer. Like so many places of one's youth, it too is no more. The creek still exists but public access does not. Population surged upward and demographics ruined what locals had enjoyed for over a hundred years. Damn the people who leave trash, break bottles, and destroy sacred places.

In the town of Kansas, Oklahoma you will find a building much like Levi's store. Dave's barber shop occupies it and offers the best haircut in town. In the middle of the street there is a hand-dug well. The history of the town's founding is like that in this book. A small man who the Indians called Little Kansas sold supplies out of a wagon that he picked up at the depot in Siloam Springs, Arkansas. We do not know the man's real name. He did not stay. My fictional Little Kansas does stay.

Many towns in the West were started by an individual with a wagon load of goods. Saint Louis, Dallas, and Denver all share similar beginnings as Kansas, Oklahoma. I have worked in and visited them all. I still choose Kansas over any of the rest.

Row, Indian Territory was a few miles north of present-day Colcord. At the time this story takes place it had hotels, stores, blacksmith, and a doctor's office. None of the businesses stand now. To many it is just the north side of Colcord. Row does have a longer history than that of Colcord. A history that you can learn about at the Talbot Museum in Colcord, Oklahoma. One day I may write about the two towns and post office theft that occurred. If the story is true, the residents of the newly formed Colcord needed a post office. So naturally they stole the one in Row and pulled it several miles to the south with horses to the new town. The residents of Row then stole it back. Least that is what I heard. Today there is no post office in Row but one in Colcord. So, Colcord won.

Orchard City was and is a real place. Today it is known as Gentry, Arkansas. One artistic liberty I did take is the telegraph wire in Orchard City. In real life the telegraph line did not arrive until a year later. My character needed it sooner, so I brought it to town sooner. I doubt anyone will care, but in case a devout Orchard City/Gentry historian reads this book I will save him or her the angry email.

Towns at that time did have night watchmen. They were not necessarily police officers. The job would not have paid the best, but the work was steady. Citizens slept better knowing someone was keeping watch against the criminal element or accidental house fires.

At a time when wood was the most common material for buildings and fire the most common heat source, town fires did occur at a high rate. Add the use of candles and kerosene lamps to the equation and the conditions were perfect for a blaze. In 1871 a fire in Chicago killed over 300 people and created over 100,000 homeless citizens. Between 1877 and 1916 Paris, Texas would burn down on three separate occasions.

Nebo too was real. Although people now know it as Gravette. Most of Benton and Washington County, Arkansas were covered in orchards. For forty years apples were the cash crop. Railroad lines carried the fruit to markets across the country. In the early twentieth century an apple blight destroyed the trees and ended the fruit dynasties. Names like Tyson, Peterson and Simmons would be the new dynasties. Chicken would become king and instead of railroads, trucks would haul the protein across the nation.

The Anti Horse Thief Association was operational in Northwest Arkansas at the time the story takes place. Eventually it would find its way to Indian Territory along with non-Indian settlers. A person would pay dues and agree to ride if called upon to retrieve stolen livestock. Sometimes the people who stole the animals did not survive the trip back. If they did not get shot by the AHTA during capture they sometimes became clumsy and managed to get their necks caught in ropes tied to oak branches.

As with any vigilante group or mob you can get a good estimate of the average I.Q. of the group by taking the total number of people divided by the I.Q. score of the dumbest individual in the group. Then move the decimal two places to the right. Point is, law abiding citizens did on occasion assist law enforcement with capturing outlaws when trivial things like jurisdictions got in the way. However, lynchings and personal vendettas did occur. My own ancestors were members of the AHTA. There were members who no doubt were honorable citizens. Some, I have my doubts their intentions were noble. My experience with people leaves me leery.

Toward the end of the book a baseball game takes place. At that time in history and up until the middle of the twentieth century most towns and communities had a baseball team. It was this nation's sport. It was played by all levels of income class and ancestral background. In Indian Territory, the game became religious. Even today more natural athletes can be found at a Kenwood softball game than at the Royal's training camp. One could argue hunting was a more popular sport; however, hunting was survival. Either for personal consumption or the marketing of the meat, hides, and feathers.

Shelby's ice cream parlor is fictional, but the Crown Hotel is real. You can see it in downtown Siloam Springs, Arkansas. It's been a while since I frequented the area but I'm sure you can find some ice cream. I know there is a good pizza joint and a bakery. If you can't find ice cream downtown there is always the Braum's on 412. I was tempted to use the original name "Hico" for the town. After researching it I discovered the town official changed the name a few years before this story takes place.

Fire, the good kind. In the book the residents used controlled burns to manage the open range and timber. Before the Cherokee settled the area, the Osage would burn the prairies and timber portions annually. This ensured a couple of things. One, new grass growth attracted elk, bison, and deer. Two, berries such as blackberries, strawberries, and huckleberries would thrive in the burnt areas. People utilized the berries but also bears. Bears love berries. Both the Osage and Cherokee harvested bears for meat, hides and lard. Bear grease had and does have many uses. People cooked with it. Mix herbs with it for healing ointments. Style hair or trade as currency for items one wanted.

By 1890 the bears were gone, killed out by market hunters. Although the practice of burning continued into the twentieth century. Population growth and land management practices changed, and the prairies have shrunk. With fire removed, brush and trees have slowly taken over. If not for cattlemen, the prairies would disappear entirely. Ironically, the bears have returned. Go bears.

About the Author

Born and raised on the Ozark Plateau. Charlie Amos grew up in the footsteps of outlaws, cowboys, and woodsmen. When he is not tending cattle and kids he is reading and writing about the American West. Years of working in agriculture, forestry, trucking, and teaching school has laid the foundation of telling our American story through relatable characters. Writing westerns for westerners, and everyone else.

He currently lives in Oklahoma with his wife, children and dog Banjo.